WILD HORSE ROBBINS

by
JACK PRICE

Copyright © 1990 by
JACK PRICE

Library of Congress
Catalog Card No. 90-81842

ISBN: 1-57579-160-9 (Paperback)
ISBN: 1-57579-161-7 (Hardcover)

ALL RIGHTS RESERVED

First Printing 1990
Second Printing 1991
Third Printing 1999
Fourth Printing 2001
Fifth Printing 2016

Printed in the United States of America
PINE HILL PRESS
A PRINT RIGHT PRINTING COMPANY
1808 N K Ave
Sioux Falls, SD 57104

WILD HORSE ROBBINS

This book is dedicated to Christina "Toots" Robbins

ACKNOWLEDGEMENTS

My sincere thanks to Mrs. Robbins. Without her, this book would not have been possible. She opened up her home, scrap books, photo albums, and boxes of magazines and pictures. She told as many stories as she could remember.

Thanks to Rita who helped me with the manuscript; to Karma for the sketch of Black Rock Butte; and a special thanks to my wife, Mavis, who never complains when I'm home in body only, while my thoughts are in Wyoming's Red Desert rounding up material to write about. Thanks also to other family members and friends for photos, other materials, and encouragement when I needed it so much.

—Jack

TABLE OF CONTENTS

Chapter 1 1

Chapter 2 9

Chapter 3 21

Chapter 4 29

Chapter 5 47

Chapter 6 63

Chapter 7 75

Chapter 1

Frank Robbins was destined to become a wild horse runner and trainer. Before he was born, an unusually mean bronc kicked the top rail off a corral, striking his father on the head and killing him. Yet, rather than hating wild horses, Frank loved them. I believe his lust to capture wild horses stemmed from a desire to break and tame them so they would be safe to be around.

Frank's father, who was also his namesake, came to Wyoming to stake out a homestead claim. Frank "Skinny" Robbins, a Kentucky gentleman gambler, arrived in the Boxelder, Wyoming, area in 1880, with a Kentucky thoroughbred stallion tied behind his wagon. The wagon was loaded with his wife, Susan, his children, and all their belongings.

The Laramie mountains looked like a good place to settle and establish a ranch. There was plenty of timber to build with and plenty of feed and water for the livestock. Wild game was plentiful; and the cold mountain streams were full of delicious fish, just waiting to be caught.

Frank Robbins, Sr., being from Kentucky, always had a race horse. He built a straightaway race track east of what is now Glenrock's city park. This is the land where his son, Frank, Jr., later built the arena for his rodeos.

During the time Frank, Sr., operated the track, cavalry officers from Fort Casper and Fort Fetterman came to race meets. They ran three heats, the best two out of three winning. The Ft. Casper teams would always insist on a $500 wager if they came. They always had very good government horses.

One year, Robbins told them he didn't have the $500, but he did have a bunch of Indian ponies he would wager. For some unexplained reason, the Ft. Casper team won the two heats at the races. Being very pleased with their racing ability, they went to the saloon to celebrate their good luck. Robbins, Sr., was a very good poker player and soon had a full-handed game going. It lasted until noon the following day, at which time the soldiers departed for Ft. Casper with their Indian ponies.

A friend of Robbins who had witnessed the whole thing told Frank he was sorry he lost the ponies. Robbins replied, "I knew I would lose them, but I did win every dollar they had." It amounted to about $3,000 — quite a sum of money at that time.

Wild Horse Frank Robbins was born November 7, 1894, on the ranch his daddy had homesteaded and built up. He was the youngest of the Robbins children, with five older brothers, Charlie, Roy, Bill, Harry, and Walter, to help and coach him. He probably learned to ride before he could walk. His sisters, Frances and Mary, no doubt, enjoyed their little brother, too.

Although Frank never knew his dad, he talked about him often, recalling many stories he had been told of his horse racing and gambling days.

Frank was just a little fellow when his mother remarried — to a man named Bill Kimball. Susan and Bill had two girls, Josephine and Topsy, and two boys, Burt and Bill. The children all attended a sod school house about a mile from their ranch. Sometimes they had to go in the summer, too. Like most boys, Frank preferred riding horses, fishing, hunting, or almost anything except going to school, especially in the summer.

Bill Kimball was a stepfather who didn't treat the Robbins boys very well. The older ones soon left home, but Frank, being the youngest, had to stick it out. After age 5, he spent a considerable part of his time by himself in a camp he had fashioned down by the creek near the ranch house. Here he taught himself to trap, hunt, fish, cook, and take care of himself, building an independence that followed him all through life. He always did his own work. In later years, if plumbing was needed on the ranch, he did it. If there was building to be done, he did that, too. It didn't always

CHAPTER 1

look like professional work, but he made do with what he had to work with.

By the time young Frank had finished grade school, he had become an expert roper and bronc rider. He began working as a cowboy and broke horses for many ranchers throughout the west.

Frank and his brother, Harry, teamed up and began following the rodeo circuit in one show after another. They won enough money to travel on, but little beyond that. An older brother, Roy "Skeeter Bill," had traveled to Hollywood and was making movies there. Frank and Harry drifted out to visit him.

Cowboys who could rope and ride like the Robbins boys had no trouble landing jobs as seconds and stunt men in the movies. Skeeter Bill was well established. He had been in many rodeos and wild west shows, working part of the time for Hoot Gibson. Skeeter also wrote poetry and songs in the true cowboy manner. The popular old cowboy song, THE STRAWBERRY ROAN, is to his credit.

The Robbins boys were all lean and lanky and dressed in traditional cowboy wear. Although Frank and Harry found steady work in Hollywood, the life soon became boring and they decided to move on, continuing to follow the rodeos. Between shows, they broke horses and eventually worked their way back home to Boxelder.

John and Mary Millar were married in Dysart, Scotland, in 1873. They came to the United States looking for land of their own so that they might raise a family. Soon after arriving in America, they headed west to Colorado, where they suffered the heartache of losing two of their children. David and Christina were buried in Colorado.

The family moved on, traveling north this time, and arrived in Glenrock, Wyoming, in 1882. John took a job working in the coal mines and went about picking a good parcel of land to homestead. An ideal spot was found where Deer Creek empties into the North Platte River, just at the northeast edge of Glenrock.

This tract of land had a rich history. It had been used as a camping grounds for different Indian tribes. Later, about 1846, it became a famous camp for emigrant wagon trains headed for Utah, Oregon, and California.

In a canyon south of Glenrock, the Mormons planted gardens. This provided food for their people as they migrated west to settle in Utah. The place still carries the name Mormon Canyon.

The Pony Express came through and established a station on the west bank of Deer Creek on what was, until recently, the Clarence Hershey place.

The first telegraph line also passed by this tract of land, and a log stockade was built to ward off hostile Indians. Later, a small village was built up on what is now Glenrock's city ball park. It was called Nuttall and consisted of about 50 houses and small dwellings.

The railroad came through in 1887, opening the territory up for mining and ranching. A portion of this land had been set aside as a hay reservation where hay was mowed and hauled to Fort Fetterman for the cavalry horses stationed there.

The hay reservation was eventually relinquished by the government, and the land was then homesteaded by John Millar. Here, a house was built of logs, using dovetail notching to fit them together.

A big, happy family was raised on the Millar ranch, including Peter, Tom, Jon, Mary Rebecca, Duvina, and Duncan, followed by another Christina. This little girl was so special to her older brothers that they often took turns carrying her around singing "toot, toot, tootsie." It didn't take long before her nickname, Toots, had firmly taken hold.

John Millar died quite young and left Mary with a big family to raise by herself. Rebecca also died young, leaving a little daughter, Jessie, whom Grandma Mary took under her wing. Jessie and Toots grew up just like sisters.

Mary Millar had to work hard raising the family. She took in wash from neighbors and cooked at the sheepshearing corrals east of town. The boys, Pete, Tom, and Jon, helped out as they became old enough to work in the mines.

CHAPTER 1

Mary Millar is remembered by many as a woman who exemplified the true pioneer spirit. Left with very little, she survived as a loving and steadfast mother, doing whatever was necessary to provide for the health and happiness of her family.

Frank Robbins became a close friend of Duncan Millar. Their common bond was horse racing. The local ranch hands would gather on Sundays and holidays to race their fastest horses. Duncan's sister, Christina, who was usually called Toots, raced, too. She was slim and pretty, and Frank took quite a shine to her. She liked him, too.

One day during a horse race, Toots was leading by a length when her bridle bit got turned in her horse's mouth. The horse, realizing that something was wrong, panicked and started running away with her. Young Robbins followed and finally overtook her and grabbed the bridle reins and brought her frightened horse to a stop. For Toots, it was Frank Robbins from then on. They began to see a lot of

The Millar Ranch eventually became home for Frank and Toots. Toots was born in the ranch house and still lives there.

each other, either riding horseback or going out to neighborhood dances with the horse and buggy. They often brought Toot's mother, Mary, to dances with them. It wasn't because they needed a chaperone, but because they enjoyed her company. It used to be customary for older people to go to dances, sitting on the side lines to watch the young ones dance. Many Sundays were spent at one of the many trout streams in the mountains. Toots and Jessie would ride off in a cloud of dust on their horses, followed by Frank and Mary in the buggy bringing the picnic dinner and the fishing tackle. They all loved to fish the mountain streams.

On May 24, 1918, Frank and Toots were married in Douglas. The knot they tied was to hold " 'til death do us part."

A short while after their honeymoon, Frank answered the call to serve in World War I. Toots dreaded the day he was to leave; but he was soon on his way to El Paso, Texas, where he received basic training as a cavalry soldier and was put to work breaking remount horses. Toots was able to visit him once while he was there.

The cavalry was the natural branch of service for Frank. He was in his natural element handling the government horses. He was on his way to Georgia with a trainload of cavalry horses destined for foreign duty when the war ended. Young Frank was so happy to be discharged, he put on his ranching clothes and left his army togs on the barracks floor. He headed for Glenrock, Wyoming, and his bride.

It didn't take Frank and Toots long to get into a cattle operation. They lived in the mountains and took care of a herd of long-horned cattle that had been shipped by rail from Texas. The lush mountain grass fattened them and, in the fall, they were rounded up and shipped to market.

Early in their married life, Frank and Toots ventured into Canada while following rodeos. The country, being very sparsely settled, caused rodeos to be few and far between, so they landed on a ranch near Gwynne, Canada. Toots cooked for the hands, and Frank broke and looked after horses.

The main Sunday entertainment for the area was ball games. People came from near and far to play ball and to

CHAPTER 1

watch the games. The word got out that young Robbins was quite a bronc stomper, so the local ranchers started bringing their outlaws and spoiled horses to the ball games. They would take up a collection by passing the hat and the money would be offered to Frank to ride the outlaw horses. He would never disappoint them. He always began his ride by throwing his hat up in the air and exciting the crowd with a wild ride. His ever-present sense of humor prevailed wherever he went. He had been described as "Will Rogers with a modified Durante-type nose."

While working on the ranch at Gwynne, Frank and Toots had the opportunity to take in the Calgary Stampede. Both entered their mounts in the parade, and Toots won a Kodak camera and Frank a pair of spurs. Frank also placed in the saddle bronc riding and calf roping events. They soon tired of Canada and returned home to Wyoming.

Eventually, Frank and Toots felt a need to get off on their own and moved to Nevada. Just off the highway near Wells, Nevada, they bought land and began building a ranch on it. Together, they went back into the timber, carrying their lunch, to cut logs. They cut all day and pulled the logs home at night with a team of mules. They lived in a tent while a house was built and later built a good set of pole corrals and a barn, too.

Using the cold water from the spring, Frank fashioned a refrigerator for Toots. He made holes in a copper pipe

Frank and Toots built this ranch house in Nevada.

so the ice-cold spring water dripped over burlap bags. The combination of the cold water, plus the evaporation process, made for quite an efficient cooler. The extra water was used for watering trees in the yard.

The Robbins raised cattle, horses, chickens, turkeys, and a few hogs on their ranch. It was here that Frank's early trapping know-how came in handy. There were coyotes, bobcats, and fox on the Arizona strip. Frank set out a trap line and made fair money selling furs from the animals he caught.

Frank was always eager to compete in any rodeo that came along. When Eley, Nevada, had a big celebration on the Fourth of July, the Robbins were there. They had a team of oxen that Frank had broken to the yoke. He entered his team and covered wagon in the parade. On the side of the wagon he had a sign which read, "Constipated, I can't pass a thing." That brought cheers and laughter from the spectators. He won second place with his parade entry, first place in saddle bronc riding, and second place in roping. Not a bad showing!

Word came that Mary, Toots' mother, was failing and help was needed back at the ranch near Glenrock. The decision to leave Nevada was a hard one. Frank and Toots had built up a nice little spread in over ten years of working on the ranch and they had done it by working together, just the two of them, but the Glenrock area also had strong ties for them.

Mrs. Wells, the local midwife, who was nursing Toots' mother, had brought both Toots and Frank into the world. They had many friends and relatives there and, besides, someone was needed to take over the Millar ranch.

The Nevada ranch was sold, and Frank and Toots came home to start the Robbins ranch at Glenrock.

Chapter 2

The dictionary defines desert as a dry, sandy area with little or no vegetation, especially wild and not lived in. This certainly describes Wyoming's Red Desert; but, contrary to what is believed, the desert is a beautiful and fascinating place. It can definitely grow on a person.

Toots Robbins is often asked how she could stand it out there. She replies, "Stand it? I loved it out there and wouldn't have been any place else."

One of the most fascinating attractions is the sand dunes, white as sugar, and almost as fine. The winds keep them drifting, shifting, and taking on different shapes.

During the winter, snow drifts over the dunes and sand drifts over the snow, burying it deeply inside the sand dunes. When spring arrives, and the sun shows off its powerful rays, the snow slowly melts into water, seeping away to a low place with a solid bottom to form a small lake. This takes place all along the ridge of sand dunes which probably extends 30 or 40 miles into the desert. Some of the lakes have water in them all summer because the snow melts slowly, buried deeply in the sand. These are excellent watering holes for horses, cattle, sheep, and wild game.

Near the sands, petrified turtles, sponges, snails, and oyster beds have been found. Fossil fish can be found on some of the higher ridges bordering the desert.

Toward the west is Steamboat Mountain, the Tables, and Boar's Tusk, all lava rock formations. To the south and west are Black Rock and Spring Butte, backed up by the leucite hills on the skyline marking the place where the coal mining camp of Superior is hidden in a deep canyon. These are also lava rock formations.

The Tables rise above the Red Desert.

Black Rock was, at one time, a hideout for the Butch Cassidy gang. They had a rope hanging down in a crevice. After getting on top of the butte and pulling the rope up behind them, they could hold off a small army from their vantage point.

There is a good spring of water near the butte. One must be wary, however, of the treacherous soap holes a short distance east of the butte. It is easy for livestock to get into them and suffocate or drown in the murky mud. They are so dangerous because they appear dry on the surface. Under a thin layer of a cracked, crispy-dry dirt crust is a hellhole of mud.

My Dad and I once pulled a mustang out of one. Just his head, front shoulders, and front legs were sticking out of the mud as he struggled for his life. His hind legs and tail were almost straight down as if he had fallen into a well. We put our lariats on him and, after much work and struggle, pulled him free. That old clay mud stuck onto his hair all summer, like cement.

Plant life on the desert is very fragile and delicate. If anything ruins the root systems, it takes an eternity for it to grow back. With topsoil restricted to small bumps and patches and with so little rainfall, a person wonders how anything ever got started growing in the first place.

CHAPTER 2

Spring brings quite an assortment of flowers, some of the most beautiful being the cactus blooms and desert roses. A sprinkling of Indian Paintbrush grows on the highest ridges. The various kinds of brush also take on pretty colors. Rabbit Brush is yellow-green. Greasewood, with its armor of sharp thorns for protection, is a major source of salt in the diet of desert animals. Even the sagebrush takes on a pretty purple-green, and gives off an indescribable aroma which really grows on you. The colors of horned toads and sand lizards blend in well with the rocks as they slither across to get out of sight. Underneath, scorpions wait to sting any curious intruder. Chipmunks scurry around, curious and almost friendly. They stay well out of reach of the human hand. The howling of coyotes at night has been a lullaby to wranglers for years as they slide down inside their bedrolls after a long day in the saddle.

Along with spring come litters of furry, cute, little coyote pups, born in litters of two to eight, with their eyes closed like their domesticated cousin, the dog. They, too, can be tamed if removed from the den before their eyes are opened. As they grow and are taken out of the den by their parents, they join in the howling with their high-pitched, immature voices, definitely singing off-key. By the time their first winter rolls around, they have matured enough so that their voices blend in with the old ones.

Badgers are also plentiful on the Red Desert, digging holes all over. It seems as if they prefer to dig in a hard-packed road or trail. Although seldom observed in daylight, their presence is readily evidenced by their freshly dug holes with a big mound of dirt nearby. The bigger the mound, the deeper the hole. Mustangs seldom step directly into a badger hole. They know, too well, where there is a mound of dirt, there is likely to be a hole. Occasionally, one will break through where a badger has dug a shallow tunnel.

Cottontails and jack rabbits are at home on the desert. The fur of the jack rabbit turns white in winter to blend with the snow for protection from predators. Cottontails keep their grayish-brown color, relying on their fleet get-away to take them down a hole to safety.

The kangaroo mouse lives in the sands. This fellow is a real oddity, carrying himself in an almost upright position on large, strong hind legs, followed by a long and equally strong tail. They hop along in much the same manner as a kangaroo. The front legs are small and are carried limply as they hop along.

Pack rats live mostly where there is a ledge of rocks. They get their name by carrying all sorts of things back to their home. They are not above raiding a camp and stealing things of absolutely no use to them and are especially attracted to shiny objects.

Of the bird population, bluebirds probably lead in beauty and in numbers, followed by magpies, blackbirds, and an occasional meadow lark.

The magpie is a pretty black and white bird with a long tail. Magpies have a preference for meat in their diet and like nothing better than to sit on the back of a sore-backed horse to pick at the sore. For this reason, they are not considered a favorite or desirable bird. Sage chickens, or grouse, are found around the springs. The young birds are tender and tasty; however, the old ones identifiable by their breast of black feathers, are as tough as boot leather.

Deer and antelope abound and can always be hunted for camp meat. This wild meat gets a bit tiresome; but, believe me, after a few months on the range, you become extremely versatile in its preparation.

This is an approximation of the conditions in the Red Desert in the heyday of Robbins. I'm sure it hasn't changed a whole lot since.

The wild horses were brought here by the Spaniards. They were not natives like the coyotes and bobcats. Centuries ago, the horses got away from the Spaniards and banded up in the wide, open spaces. Later, the pioneers came west bringing with them thoroughbreds and many other fine breeds of horses. Many of these also escaped and went to run with the Spanish mustangs. This greatly improved the blood lines of the mustangs.

CHAPTER 2

The Indians trapped them and broke them to ride and pull a travois. Some early settlers would crease them as a method of capturing them. Creasing involved shooting them at the top edge of the neck. This would stun the horse long enough to get a rope on him. Many more horses were killed through this process than captured.

Some ranchers lost good stock to the wild herds as the stallions lured their mares away in the night. Many ordered their ranch hands to shoot any mustangs they saw. Others hated the idea. It was too much like murder, although they conceded that one horse ate as much as two cows.

In a report made as territorial governor in 1889, the late Senator Francis E. Warren estimated there were four horses for each human inhabitant as compared to 28 sheep and 34 cattle per capita in the territory. No class of livestock is as hardy or free from disease as horses. Horses will always paw through the snow for grass. They will trot for miles to a spring for water when it is scarce. The range furnishes all the necessary food for growing horses. They graze closer to the ground than other livestock so an abundance of feed is always available to them. The Wyoming range is a natural home for horses. Here, they are developed in a more uniform manner than anywhere else in the country.

As the herd of mustangs grazed, scattered out in the bottom of a brushy draw, a stiff breeze blew from the north. It was a cold spring breeze and the horses had moved to the draw for protection. The keeper of the harem, a palomino stallion, had taken up a position on a little knoll as if to challenge anyone to a game of king of the hill. He had picked this elevated spot to be where he could protect the mares from any threat. There were always young stallions waiting to take mares for their own and older ones trying to add to their harems. There was also the ever present fear of riders who would like to corral them or get close enough to rope them, or those who would chase them, just to see them run.

The origin of this stallion is unknown, but palominos are as scarce as hen's teeth among the mustangs. He had probably gotten away from some rancher who would never recapture him now that he had a taste of the freedom of the wild. The old boy had many battle scars, proof of his determination, and a large bunch of mares, proof of his ability to take on any challenger and end up victorious.

On this cold, windy day, his lead mare, a beautiful light sorrell mare, began acting restless, trying to leave the others. Several times the stud trotted down and turned her back. With his neck stretched out, his nose nearly touching the ground, and his ears laid back, he would nudge her back into the herd. Finally, she just walked off, wouldn't turn back. He let her go without a fight. He knew when to quit.

The sorrel mare slowly picked her way up over the ridge into a grassy hollow and started to graze. This was a familiar spot to her. She had come here before to foal.

Mares get away from the herd to foal. Quite often, another mare about ready to foal, will claim a newborn colt. Even a dry mare who isn't with foal, will claim it. The motherly instinct is very strong in horses.

As darkness settled in over the Red Desert, it got colder and began to snow. By morning, the ground was white. This was a poor time for a colt to be born. The foaling process continued despite the conditions. As soon as the little fellow was born, his mother was up rubbing his wet, golden coat with her nose to give him warmth and stimulation. He let out a faint nicker, and the mother nickered back to encourage him. Soon, he was trying to get up. He was a strong colt, but those long, spindly legs would be hard to coordinate for awhile. First, he raised his head, then got his front feet propped up ahead of him. Pushing with his hind legs, he stood up, lost his balance, and sprawled head first into the snow.

With his mother's nudging and nickering encouragement, he soon tried it again. After several attempts, he was able to stand and, after much searching and nuzzling along both sides of his mother, he finally found the mare's teats and took on a good fill of milk. The milk was warm and rich, warming his insides, helping to fight off the cold. Only a good, strong colt could survive these conditions.

CHAPTER 2

By midmorning, the clouds had disappeared, allowing the sun to do her stuff to old Mother Earth. The snow melted quickly, leaving the feeling of spring in the air once again.

Desert Dust, as he was to become known, did a lot of sleeping in the sun the first few days of his life. He grew and became strong and more active as the days went by. One day, as he ventured much too far from his mother, he saw a furry animal, not nearly as tall as he was. Deciding it would be a fun plaything, he started chasing it. The animal didn't really run; it just moved aside. The colt took another run at it. By this time, another one had come into the picture and soon they were doing the chasing. The mare must have smelled the coyotes or somehow sensed danger to her baby. She came to investigate. With flying hoofs and bared teeth, she chased those hungry coyotes away from her foal.

After a few days, the mare took her colt back to join the herd. Her yearling was glad to see her mother, but was real curious about the little golden-colored colt who had taken her place. She cautiously went up to give him a smell. Little Desert Dust opened and closed his mouth as if gumming or chewing on something. This signals immunity from abuse or harm from other horses until they are mature enough to fight for themselves.

The old stud proudly pranced down for a closer look at his newest offspring, the first of the season. The little fellow had all the color and the markings of his father. By this time, his ears had started to curl down and get brittle. They had been frozen that cold morning when he was born. Eventually, the tips would fall off, making him a crop-eared horse.

Soon, there were many new colts for little Desert Dust to play and romp with. He was the only palomino, probably because his mother was the only sorrel in the bunch. The rest of the mares were brown, bay, and black. Sorrel mares seem to have the best luck getting palomino colts from a pally stud.

The wild colt grew fast. His long, spindly legs became steady and well-muscled above hard, well-shaped hoofs. The type of terrain and soil have a lot to do with the formation of the feet. Colts born on rocky, hard ground develop small, hard feet, as opposed to those born and raised in sandy, soft soil. Horses growing up in the sand dunes area have a tendency to have flat feet, giving them a definite advantage for running in the sand. The land around Dobe Town, where Desert Dust grew up, is very rocky and rough, and helped to develop a nearly perfect horse.

At just about sunup on a midsummer morning, the old herd stallion gave a shrill whistle out of his nostrils, the signal to alert the entire herd to danger. Mothers quickly called their colts to their sides and, just as quickly, the whole herd was off in a cloud of dust, running at top speed. The sorrel mare took the lead with the golden colt at her heels. The rest of the mares and colts followed close behind with the herd stallion bringing up the rear. If there were any slow ones or stragglers, he bit them on the rump to make them keep up.

This was Desert Dust's first experience of running with the herd and he really enjoyed it. It also scared him a little, wondering what they were running from. After about a mile of running, he saw his mother look to the right and he looked to the right, also. There he saw it. A lone running horse with something sitting upright on its back. This was the first of many encounters he would have with wild horse runners. Keeping up with the fast pace of his mother wasn't easy as she ran down a long ridge and ended up in a network of canyons where she skillfully lost the rider. The herd continued to run, but at a slower speed, until they were sure they had given the horse runner the slip.

After that, they walked well into the night. Morning found them in very rough country, far from their familiar range. Here they took refuge with plenty of time to rest and graze. After a few days, they slowly worked their way back to their home range.

Fall came, cooling the weather slowly and giving way to winter. As the snow fell and the wind blew, the horses turned their backs to the storm drifting along with the wind until they came to a deep draw where the brush was tall enough to afford shelter. There they waited out the Wyoming blizzard. The snow accumulated knee-deep and then crusted. Only the seasoned horses could paw it to expose grass for grazing. The colts kept close to their mothers to graze where they pawed away the crusted snow.

Along with the cold weather came the weaning of the colts. The mares refused to let them suck, making them feel badly abused. Soon the mothers' milk dried up so they could utilize their food to maintain their body flesh and prepare for the arrival of new foals when spring came again.

After the snow, the wild horses had no need to go to the spring for water. They ate snow. Most of their grazing was done on high ridges where the snow had blown off. Occasionally, a herd of wild horses would get caught on a high ridge, where the snow would drift, surrounding them with deep drifts. Horses are afraid to go into deep snow. When it gets about belly deep, they fear getting stuck. Consequently, when the grass is all grazed off, they will starve unless rescued.

Many ranchers know where these trouble spots are located and break trails for the herds. A good saddle horse trusts his master and can be led through very deep snow. The wild ones need only one track to follow, leading to better grazing and shelter from the wind.

With the arrival of spring, the mustangs began shedding their winter coats, a process that takes many weeks, but leaves them with a coat of short, sleek, and shiny hair.

Desert Dust was a handsome yearling, nearly as tall as his mother, with a beautifully golden-colored body, white mane and tail, a white stripe in his face, and four stockinged feet. He lived his second year much the same as the first, with a few skirmishes with wild horse runners, and an occasional false alarm as a sheepherder or cowboy rode through the countryside on his rounds. The mustangs always ran at the sight of a rider.

In the spring of his second year his life began to change. He was reaching maturity and no longer romped and played with the colts. He began showing interest in the mares. About the time he had one of them convinced he was a pretty nice fella, the old herd stallion came at him with flying hoofs and bared teeth to drive him out of the herd. He must have thought he was being treated badly; but, try as he did, he

Desert Dust.

couldn't get past his own father to get back into the herd. He finally gave up trying and threw in with a couple other young studs who had been kicked out of other herds.

These young stallions band together because they don't like being alone. They are curious, but cautious, and can run like the wind. The palomino ran with the young studs for two years, often trying to fight his way into a herd to steal a mare or two. He didn't succeed, but he got a lot of battle experience and developed his muscles for the day he would make the big challenge, perhaps with the old palomino herd stallion himself.

The spring he turned four, he ranged close to the spring waiting for the wild herds to come in to drink. Each day brought several challenges with older wild stallions who were seasoned fighters. He wouldn't give up. He knew he would eventually win.

His lucky day came when a herd of 13 mares with colts trotted down to the spring. They were followed by a bay stallion who had control of his harem. He was ready to fight when he was challenged by Desert Dust.

CHAPTER 2

A furious battle followed. The bay, an older, more experienced battler, and the palomino, a young, active, and determined horse reared high into the air coming down biting, squealing, and striking at each other with their front hoofs. Next the bay wheeled, kicking Desert Dust in the side. The palomino was quick to recover and pounced on the bay to bite him hard on top of the withers. The battle raged on for most of the day. The bay's age began to show as he slowly tired. Desert Dust kept fighting and kicking mercilessly, finally kicking the old bay out of the herd. The old stallion didn't give up easily, but hung around at a safe distance, trying to lure some of the mares away. Some of the mares didn't like being dominated by this new horse. They would gladly have gone with their old leader, but Desert Dust herded them together, putting his head close to the ground, his nose extended forward, and his ears laid back. They knew he could be very ferocious if they didn't obey. The old stallion finally drifted on, realizing defeat.

Desert Dust had it made. This is what being a wild stallion is all about.

Chapter 3

Frank heard about the wild horses on the Red Desert that could be had for the taking *if* you could capture them. Not one to pass up a challenge and, with as much horse know-how as anybody in the country, he headed for the desert. Toots stayed at home on the ranch to care for her elderly mother.

In the fall of 1935 he arrived in the desert north of Wamsutter with a broken axle on his Model A car and, as he put it, "a saddle even a junkman wouldn't want." He had no horse. "I had to catch a horse before I had one to ride," he lamented.

After much scouting and exploring the dry, parched country which mostly contained sagebrush, sand, and rocks, he came upon an artesian well where hundreds of horses were watering. Some oil company had drilled for oil and struck a good vein of flowing water, leaving it to form a small pond, a real oasis in the desert. The artesian well was many miles from any other watering hole, so it was an ideal place to build a trap. The mustangs would take quite a few chances before traveling 15 or 20 miles to the next watering hole. They just drank once a day, and the heat of the desert creates quite a thirst in the broom tails.

The trap was a strong corral of cable and wire, using railroad ties for posts. Frank encircled the watering hole with the corral, leaving a single opening near a hide-out just outside the gate where he would hide until the horses were all inside.

These horses had been run off water by horsemen trying to rope them for so long that they had gotten so they would go for water only at night. The horses came in bunches, usually 5 to 20 head, depending upon the strength and fighting ability of the stallion. Wild horse herds seldom mix together.

To do so would mean immediate, furious battle between the stallions. Stallions are very protective of their harems and dominate them until they are too old to fight. The two-year-old studs are kicked out of the herd as they reach maturity and begin to compete for the mares. These young studs band together until they find an old stallion they can whip and take over his harem of mares.

Frank's patience paid off the next night. After closing the gate on the unsuspecting mustangs, he quietly slipped away to camp. He didn't want to be around when the horses discovered their fate. They would panic, and the dark, quiet night would give way to stampede and sparks as metal wire stretched against metal cable. He would return in the morning after they had settled down.

After a breakfast of sourdough hot cakes and antelope chops, he returned and was pleased to see a brown mare in the first bunch he caught. She looked, to his experienced eye, as if she had been handled some and upon catching her, he found she was green broke. Frank was no longer afoot. Nobody knew where the mare came from. She had evidently gotten away from someone and taken up with the mustangs.

The trap at the artesian well produced well, and the horses were averaging $18 a head. Most were sold to rodeos. Some he took back to the ranch near Glenrock. Eventually, the horses got wise to the trap and found another watering hole. Frank had to search, again, for a new, isolated watering hole to construct his next trap.

Winter was fast approaching as Frank began work on the corral at Flat Spring. This spring bubbled clear, cold water out in the middle of nowhere and was also a popular watering hole for the broom tails. One of the first things Frank did here was to build a dugout cabin.

Frank made regular trips back to Glenrock to visit and take care of business, then back to the desert he would go. He worked alone much of the time, but had Walt Turner help build the cabin. He picked the south slope of a steep, sandy knoll to dig into. The front was faced up with railroad ties and the roof was plank with dirt on top. The floor was dirt;

CHAPTER 3

but, with a little sprinkling of water and a whole bunch of walking on, it was almost like cement. It was a nice, comfortable place, warm in the winter and cool in the summer.

Once again, Frank's trapping experience stood him well. After the weather cooled in the fall and the trapping of horses was no longer successful, he would trap coyotes and badgers, selling the furs to pay expenses through the winter. Just as soon as spring arrived, he was back building and repairing the water traps and corrals.

Besides the corrals at the well and Flat Spring, he built corrals at Chain Lakes, Eagles Nest, and Sand Lake. When the horses got wise and quit drinking at one trap, he would move to another. Sometimes, he would go to a watering hole where he didn't have a corral and rope the horses after they had filled up with water. They weren't too hard to catch that way, but it was slow going, only catching one at a time.

This was about the time he acquired the name "Wild Horse" Robbins. About that same time he also began thinking about using an airplane to corral horses. They could be brought in from miles around in big bunches by herding them from the air.

Spring of the year brings many happy surprises to the Red Desert. Mother Nature is always busy bringing about new life, whether it be animal, plant or insect. One warm spring morning, Frank rode out to check on the whereabouts of his horses. Before Toots was expecting him to return, he rode into camp, carefully dismounted and took two tiny badger kittens out of his leather jacket pockets. They were the cutest little things you could ever expect to see.

The Robbins kept them, feeding them milk, first with an eye dropper, then using a baby bottle, They gave one to the lady who ran the Wamsutter Hotel and kept the other as their own pet, naming him Silver. He made a nice pet and loved to be handled and petted. He enjoyed playing with the dogs and cats and ate right along with them. When almost full-grown, he dug his own burrow behind the camp and slept in that. He would always be in camp in the morning, usually waking Robbins up by pulling on his bed blanket. He didn't, however, make friends with strangers.

Frank Robbins became known as Wild Horse Robbins.

Silver could hear a vehicle or rider coming long before anyone else could. He would perk up his little ears and be restless long before anyone showed up.

Silver's favorite treat was a ride in the truck where he would lie on his back with all four stubby legs in the air asking Toots to scratch his tummy. Frank worried that he might be run over when they had him in town so they took him to the harness shop to have a harness made. The harness maker could certainly fashion a harness for him, but he needed

CHAPTER 3

his measurements and the badger wouldn't let him touch him. Frank had to do the honors.

One day, Frank and Toots went to town, leaving Silver at camp. When they returned, he was nowhere to be found. Frank rode out and called for him, but he never did show up. He had grown up to be a beautiful silver badger, and, not being really wild, must have been easily shot or trapped by some fur trader. Frank and Toots lost a good little friend that day.

Superior is located at the west edge of the Red Desert. It was a rip-roarin' coal mining camp in the 1930s and early 40s, operating several mines with miners working in shifts around the clock. The men worked under union contract and were paid quite well. Most of the coal was used to fire the engines of the Union Pacific Railroad as the railroad owned the mining operation. The miners earned several weeks of vacation each year, and some of them couldn't pass up the opportunity to try to capture a Red Desert mustang on their vacation.

One such miner had accumulated a small herd of horses. Some he had taken from the wild bunches, and some were questionable as to how he got them. He had a stallion that closely resembled Steamboat Bill's breed of horses. Bill had been heard to say that if he ever caught the coal miner riding that horse, he would make sure he never stole another colt from him.

Having finished work at Chilton's Ranch when the spring work was done, my Dad and two brothers, Don and Short, were looking for work. They heard about a coal miner who was trying to get an outfit together to run horses. Dad contacted him and found out he wanted to gather his branded horses and brand the colts, then move a corral he said he had at the 12 Mile Spring to a place called Coal Spring Draw. There was a small vein of coal with a seepage of water coming out of it. A few horses watered there in the spring of the year, but it was dry by mid-summer.

It didn't take long to gather the branded horses. Then Dad and the boys were hauled to 12 Mile, along with the proper tools to disassemble the corral. The coal miner would return in a few days to move the corral to Coal Spring Draw. The corral at 12 Mile was actually a water trap, completely enclosing the watering hole within the confines of the corral. Any animals watering there would have to be inside the trap to get a drink.

Dad and the boys began tearing down the corral, rolling up the hundreds of yards of wire and cable, digging up posts, many of which were railroad ties, and piling them up neatly for easy loading on the truck when their new boss returned.

One evening, as their job neared completion, they were eating their supper when in rattled a rickety Model A Ford truck. Jumping out of it before it even came to a stop was a long-legged, raw-boned fellow dressed in Levis and cowboy boots, and definitely looking mad. He said, "This is my corral. Why are you tearing it down?" Dad told him about the coal miner and moving the corral to Coal Spring. He said, "You tell that SOB if he expects to keep up with me he will have to keep his head above ground."

With that, he drove away saying nothing more about the corral. They had just met Frank Robbins. Dad told the coal miner about their encounter and he denied the corral belonged to Robbins. Dad thought it remarkable, though, that he kept looking over his shoulder the whole time they were moving it.

As the corral was nearing completion, Dad got to thinking. If this guy was a little bit shady, maybe he should draw up his wages and not let him get too far ahead of him. There were no wages forthcoming. Dad took the coal miner to court, but both he and his wife testified they hadn't agreed to pay wages. One could lie as fast as the other. Dad even suspected the judge was a relative. Dad and the boys had worked and used their own horses and all they got out of it was what they ate.

After the trial, Dad was at the wholesale house where he bought feed for the saddle horses. The coal miner walked in wearing a big grin. Dad was a small man in stature, but a feisty little Irishman. It didn't take him long to wipe the

CHAPTER 3

grin off the miner's face. Dad hit him once and he turned his back, wanting no more.

The next day Dad and the boys rode out and took over the corral at Coal Spring. Squatter's rights, they figured. The coal miner didn't show up there again, but they hadn't seen the last of him.

During the early days of wild horse running, the Robbins camped in tents or makeshift shelters, usually sleeping on the ground, using hay for a mattress. Now, this wasn't too hard on an old cowboy who had been raised in roundup camps on the range, but Frank decided Toots needed a better life. She had joined Frank on the desert after her mother died and helped him wherever she could. She never dug any post holes, but would hold the posts straight while Robbins tamped them in. They were a very close couple, doing everything together, being separated only be absolute necessity. Often

During the early days of horse running, the Robbins lived in make-shift shelters.

they lived in a tent or a makeshift shelter. Frank decided to build a camper on the back of his truck.

Beginning with hardwood bows fastened to the truck box, he then stretched canvas over them in much the same way as a sheep camp is built. He put a little stove in it, built a cupboard, a fold-down table, and finished it off with a bed with a real mattress. This would be a real comfortable camp on wheels to make desert living more enjoyable. Toots put her stamp of approval on it and began looking forward to trying it out.

Spring came early and Frank was anxious to get back out to the desert and his mustangs. Spurred on by a beautiful Wyoming sunrise, Frank and Toots loaded up the truck and headed for the Red Desert.

So preoccupied with thoughts of the desert were the Robbins, they forgot about the railroad trestle crossing the road near their ranch. Too late, they realized what had happened. With an ear-splitting crack, the bows and canvas were broken off about even with the top of the truck cab. There wasn't enough clearance to let the camper pass.

Frank let loose with a string of cuss words and got out to survey the damage. The framework was ruined, but it was fixable. He made a quick trip into town to purchase new canvas and bows and, by evening, it was good as new. They took the east road out of the ranch this time and headed for the Red Desert with renewed enthusiasm.

Later, Robbins built a camp wagon on the order of a sheep-camp-on-rubber to pull behind his truck. This was much better than the camper. Toots could move the camp while Frank was moving the horses from place to place. He always stayed close enough to help her if she needed him. A sudden downpour of rain on the desert will bring almost any vehicle to a halt.

Chapter 4

As Robbins busily dug post holes and swatted deer flies and sand gnats at Wilson Draw, he thought that this could well be his most successful wild horse corral. The weather was hot and dry and the post holes dug hard; he would have become discouraged except for the gut feeling he had about this corral.

The mail plane flew past the camp regularly and came close, tipping its wings, first one way, then the other, as if in greeting to the only sign of human habitation for 40 miles.

Frank's saddle horses were enjoying a much needed rest, grazing on good grass and receiving a generous portion of oats every day. He rode them just enough to keep them in shape. They would be well rested and ready to run the mustangs when the corral was finished.

Toots was in a camp tucked away in a draw, out of sight of any mustangs grazing the countryside. Frank didn't want those horses to know he was building a corral or that he was anywhere around. If a herd found the camp, they would never come close to it again.

The camp was an important part of the wild horse round-up. Three square meals a day were necessary to keep the wranglers working. Toots had a way of making a banquet out of the simplest of foods. Antelope were easy to obtain as they watered at the spring. They provided the main source of meat. Due to the lack of refrigeration, the meat was kept in sacks, well covered with tarps and blankets in the daytime to insulate it from the hot, desert sun. At night, it was taken out of the sacks and hung out in the cool night air. Meat could be kept for up to a week if it was kept out of the sun in this manner.

Working in their sheep-camp-on-rubber, Toots prepared meals fit for a king.

CHAPTER 4

When the corral was finally finished, Wild Horse Robbins went to Rock Springs to hire a couple of hands to help with the roundup. Cowboys with wild horse running experience weren't easy to come by so he was gone for several days. He located one experienced wrangler soon after he arrived in town. That fellow had a friend looking for a job, but he hadn't seen him for a couple of days. They finally located him in the South Pass Saloon, slightly drunk. Frank knew he would be sober by the time they reached camp. Once there, there would be no booze available. He knew this guy was a good hand who would do a good job if sober and astride a good saddle horse.

The Maverick House Hotel was the next stop, a favorite flophouse for ranch hands and coal miners. The proprietor, an old-timer of the Rock Springs area, known as Dad Teeters, was a short, stocky, bald-headed man with a good sense of humor. He watched as the two wranglers hauled out their saddles and bedrolls to load into the Robbins truck.

The road to the horse camp was a two-track, rough trail, made partly by vehicles and partly by animals of the desert. The hand he had picked up in the saloon suffered with every bump in the road. The sun was low on the horizon, and the shadows were long by the time the old truck bounced into camp.

After supper, Robbins explained the lay of the land to the newly-hired wranglers, telling them all about the corral and the many herds of mustangs he had seen while he was building it.

Frank was up at daybreak to wrangle the saddle horses from a grassy draw where they were grazing. Toots soon had sourdough hot cakes browning on the griddle. Frank matched up horses and riders according to the way he had the roundup planned. The hand with the longest, hardest run to make was mounted on a horse with plenty of speed, plus plenty of bottom, or staying power. The riders assigned closer to the corral needed fast horses, but not necessarily long-winded mounts.

After riding over to view the corral, they knew just what was expected of them. They rode out in search of a herd

Robbins waits for a wild one to rope.

CHAPTER 4

of about 15 mares and colts led by a beautiful, buckskin stud. Frank had seen this bunch several times while building the corral, but he doubted if they were on to the trap. They ranged around Black Rock Butte and the 12 Mile Spring. He wanted that stallion pretty bad. He had already imagined he would look pretty good under that old A fork saddle of his.

They rode west, stopping at the top of several high hills to survey the area in search of the herd. They finally found the buckskin and his harem of mares about 15 miles from the corral.

After instructing the riders on their positions and sending the best horse to the far side of them for the most advantageous spot to spook them towards the corral, Robbins slowly made his way back to the corral. He wanted to be there, on a fresh horse, in case the herd managed to avoid the trap. He would be ready to rope one, possibly the stud.

As he rode back to the corral, he continually checked back over his shoulder as to which way they went when the wild bunch started running. Experience had taught him that they don't always go the way you plan.

Soon there was a long string of dust, assuring Robbins that his wranglers had them started towards the corral. Near the end of one wing of the corral, Frank tied his horse to a sagebush and took up a look out on a little knoll that afforded him a good view of the canyon.

The mustangs were strung out and really running. They were heading in the general direction of the corral when, all of a sudden, they caught the smell of the second rider and turned off the ridge into the draw to the south. The second rider stayed out of sight, but now the first rider would have to try to turn them back towards the corral. This would test his skill and the running ability of the saddle horse Robbins had assigned him to ride.

Dust was about all Wild Horse Robbins could see, but it told the story to this veteran mustanger. He watched as the wrangler rode wide, hoping the mares and colts would tire and turn from him. After about a ten mile run, they slowly turned back towards the corral. The second rider had cut across to where he could take them up when they got back even with him. By this time, the first rider's horse was ready for a break.

The wild bunch put on a new burst of speed when they spotted the rider mounted on a fresh horse. They kept running in the direction of the corral, though, where Frank sat astride his fresh horse.

Wild Horse Robbins felt the adrenaline rising as the herd approached the corral. He was prepared to help bring them in and rode slowly, carefully out of sight and downwind of the wild horses. He heard the steady, familiar drone of the mail plane approaching the camp. Just as Frank rode out of hiding to turn the herd down the trail, that mail plane flew over at about 100 feet and tipped its wings in friendly salute.

The wild horses didn't even notice Robbins. They were so frightened by the plane, they scattered in every direction. The pilot had no idea that his friendliness had brought havoc to this nearly successful roundup.

Determined to bunch the horses and bring them back, Frank put his horse to a dead run. After a couple of miles, it was evident that it was not to be so he fell right in behind that beautiful buckskin stallion. The buckskin had run about 25 miles now and beginning to show signs of tiring. Robbins, mounted on a fresh horse, was gaining steadily on the stud, nearing roping distance of this prize piece of horse flesh. Building a big loop as he rode, he could feel the bits of dirt and rocks the flying hoofs of this fleet-footed animal were kicking up.

He swung the loop, once, twice, and let it go with accuracy that only comes with years of experience, settling it neatly over the head, quickly taking up the slack in the rope. The stud lunged as he hit the end of the rope, nearly taking Frank's steed off its feet. The wild stallion wasn't easy to bring to a halt. He kept lunging, squealing, and pawing the air, trying to break away to freedom. The Manila hemp rope held. Soon, the other wranglers rode up and helped haze him to the corral where he was carefully examined for brands, blemishes, and defects. None was found. He was

CHAPTER 4

just as beautiful and perfect as he had appeared in the wild. This isn't always the case with wild horses.

Although the roundup had been unsuccessful, this day was very important in the life of Robbins. If the horses were that afraid of the plane, he figured, why not use one to round them up? It would take a special type of pilot, one with super flying skills, a little on the daredevil side, and who knew something about horses. He couldn't shake the idea, and was soon on his way to town to locate such a pilot. Making the rounds of airports in Rock Springs, Rawlins, and Casper, he visited with many pilots who all agreed it would be tricky and dangerous flying. The name of Everette Hogan came up as someone who could certainly do the job if he could be persuaded to take the risk.

Robbins contacted Hogan and made a deal to fly out to the Red Desert and give it a whirl. He also made a trip out to our camp at Coal Spring to see if we wanted to take part in the first aerial roundup.

Just after sunrise, the steady drone of the single engine, tandem Piper Cub was heard winging its way across the Red Desert. Frank had evidently given Hogan a good set of directions to the camp, tucked away in a draw, and the corral, camouflaged and hidden so well in another draw. He arrived right on target, setting down in a cloud of dust on a little salt sage flat. Salt sage grows about two inches tall and doesn't make a big hump with its root system like regular sagebrush does. This area was perfect for landing a small plane.

My Dad, my brother, Short, and I had ridden over from our camp the day before to be on hand, well rested with fresh saddle horses.

Not long after Hogan arrived, the plane was refueled and back in the air. This time, Wild Horse Robbins was also in the plane. Hogan, a specialist in aviation, and Frank, a professional mustanger, were teamed up to corral horses on a large enough scale to make it pay.

Hogan wasn't long in rounding up the first bunch, diving at them and heading them towards the corral. They were

Using an airplane, wild mustangs could be herded for miles in large groups.

Pilot Everette Hogan tried to circle the horses to bring them back to the corral.

CHAPTER 4

headed almost perfectly, but missed the wings of the corral by about 100 feet. By the time Hogan could see they were missing the corral, it was too late for him to maneuver the plane to turn them. He tried to circle and bring them back, but they had seen the trap and would not be brought back to it. After several more attempts, the plane had corralled only a few horses. Robbins didn't give up. It wasn't his nature to give up. From the air and with what was happening on the ground, he could see that the corral just wasn't working. It would be necessary to redesign the corral and use the advantage of this bird's-eye view to find the perfect location.

With this in mind, Frank and Hogan logged many miles in the air, searching for a location to build a new, hidden corral. One day, just at the north edge of the Red Strip, he spotted a cluster of tall chalk buttes with many horse trails leading right between the two tallest of the white buttes. Further examination revealed that the horses from northwest of there followed this trail between the buttes. These horses could be brought from the Killpecker Sand Dunes, Buffalo Hump, and Black Rock Butte very easily. From the other direction, they could be driven from the Chain Lakes, Wilson Draw, and the area of the artesian well. The Chalk Buttes were well located in the middle of wild horse range.

Miles of cable and wire, plus piles of posts, would be needed to build a corral this size. It would also take plenty of manpower. World War II had taken the majority of the hands off the range so it was difficult to hire help.

The war had left our wild horse camp at 12 Mile Springs short handed, too. We were building our corral when my two older brothers, Chuck and Don, were called to the service. This left me and my brothers, Short and Sweed, to help Dad. Jean, my youngest, sister, was there, too. Mom had died just a year earlier and Jean chose to come out to camp rather than be alone much of the time at our house in Superior.

We were about half done with our corral when Wild Horse Robbins pulled into our camp in a Model A Ford truck loaded with posts and wire. He was headed for Chalk Buttes and asked us to throw in with him. He laid out his plan for aerial herding into his redesigned corral and drew a diagram, using a stick to sketch it in the dry dirt outside our tent. The wings of this corral would nearly encircle the buttes, each one ending behind a knoll where a rider could easily stay out of sight of the mustangs until they were well within the enclosure of the wings. He wanted to use our day herd as decoys in the wings of the corral.

This looked like a good setup to us. We agreed to go down and help him, although we were rather tired of building corrals by this time.

School time was approaching rapidly so Jean and Sweed were taken to Superior to be on hand on the opening day. Two days later, we were putting a pack on our little mare, Lady, and getting ready for a trek across the Red Strip to Chalk Buttes. We took our small tent, our bedrolls, clothing, and a few other necessities. We didn't have to take any food

Left to right: Jack Price, Jake Price, Ed Buctan, Short Price, and Frank Robbins with his back to the camera.

CHAPTER 4

or utensils, though. Toots Robbins was out there, and her reputation preceded her. We would be eating with them.

We had a good-sized day herd built up – about 20 head, including the saddle horses. Some of the last ones caught were still plenty spooky, and this was only increased when they saw the mare with the pack on her back. We got out of there at a lively clip. Luckily, they got started in the right direction. Dad and Short got them stopped just before they crossed the Black Rock Wash. I was leading the pack mare, and we were considerably slower. By the time I arrived, they had quieted down so we turned the pack mare loose with the herd and let them graze for a good hour in the lush grass growing in the lowlands of the draw.

It was nearly sundown by the time we reached the Red Strip. This was my first look at it. The ground is very red, and the soil is different from anything I have ever seen. It is crumbly and soft. Horses sink into it up to their ankles. This will tire a saddle horse very quickly. Luckily, it is only a little more than a mile across.

From the Strip, it wasn't far to Chalk Buttes. We were there by sundown. It was easy to see how this place got its name. The buttes showed up stark white as the sun set on them. They rose about 200 feet above the desert floor.

Frank had constructed a holding corral for the day herd. We put them into it after they had watered at the dugout. Dad and Frank went about setting our tent up while Short and I cared for the saddle horses. By the time we were finished, it was dark. Mrs. Robbins had supper ready. We were really looking forward to this. We washed up outside the camp wagon and went inside to meet Mrs. Robbins. She was a very pleasant appearing woman; seemed quiet to me. She had prepared a meal fit for a king. The pie she had baked reminded me of home before mother passed away.

After supper, we sat around the campfire with Wild Horse Robbins and visited. He told us more about the plans for the corral and related many of his wild horse adventures. He spoke in a low tone of voice, seeming almost to whisper at times. One had to listen closely not to miss anything.

Left to right: Short Price, Everette Hogan, Jake Price, Frank "Wild Horse" Robbins, Toots Robbins, and Jack Price. Note the sheep-camp-on-rubber in the background.

I was a 16-year-old boy sitting at the campfire of a bona fide legend, Wild Horse Robbins. I wasn't missing a thing!

It must have been midnight when we finally turned in. Anyway, it was a short night. We had the day herd out to graze before sunup. They hadn't had much to eat the day before, with the traveling, so we let them take on a good fill.

To the northwest of the buttes, the land lay fairly level and open for a couple of miles. The soil was sandy and wild rice grass grew in bunches in this type of soil. The horses really liked it. The seed is just like grain, which they did very well on. It brought a nice shine to their coats. Most of the time, we just let the day herd graze, checking on them once in awhile to see that they didn't stray too far.

We were putting in long days building the corral, working from daylight until dark. The pile of posts was getting

CHAPTER 4

smaller, as was the supply of cable and wire. It was plain to see we would need additional materials to finish the job.

Frank decided to take the material from his corral at Chain Lakes. He had a couple of corrals that were closer to Chalk Buttes, but he didn't want to tear them down. The herds were wise to his corral at Chain Lake so it had to be the one to go.

Before daylight, Frank and Dad rattled out of camp in the old truck, headed east for a long day of hard work. The sun was quite a long ways up in the sky when they arrived at the Chain Lakes. The railroad tie posts had to be dug out and loaded by hand. The cable was rolled into coils so heavy it took both men to load them onto the truck. The lunch they had along was welcome as the old sun was directly over head. After a short rest, they continued their task, finishing up with the loading just at sundown.

Both men relaxed as they headed back with their much-needed cargo. As the old truck labored under the load, the two seasoned ranchers let their conversation drift from wild horses to fishing. Both loved to fish and, I expect, they both told about "the big ones that got away" as they bounced along the two-track road.

They started planning a fishing trip and had just about agreed upon a stream where they were sure to catch some whoppers, when, all of a sudden there was a snap; and the old truck ground to a halt. It didn't take long to discover a broken axle. Miles from civilization. They started walking, both wearing high-heeled cowboy boots, surely not the most comfortable footwear for a long walk.

They started out together, but long-legged Robbins was soon way ahead of Dad. Frank finally yelled back, "Just stay on the road, Jake, and keep walking. I'll come back and pick you up."

They kept walking into the night. Dad said he had no idea how far ahead Frank was, but he knew it was many, many miles to the horse camp. He rested several times; and finally a car light appeared, slowly winding, turning, and bumping along the sagebrush road toward him. Robbins had walked to the Red Desert Ranch where he got one of the hands to haul him back to pick up Dad.

It was well past midnight when they drove into the Chalk Buttes camp and told us what had happened. Toots had kept the stew warm in the Dutch oven over a hot bed of coals. They both ate like they feared there would be no tomorrow. Next morning, they doctored their blisters before going back after the loaded truck.

The post holes dug hard at Chalk Buttes. Most of them had to be chipped out with a spud bar, then cleaned out with a sand shovel. They all had to be tamped in, using a tamping bar, making certain the bottom was solid before continuing to fill with dirt and then tamping, again, until the hole was full. After what seemed like an eternity, the corral was almost finished; and a date had been set for Everett Hogan to fly in again.

These were exciting days for me. There was a chance I might get my first plane ride. The corral looked fine, too. We felt that it couldn't miss.

Hogan's plane looked like a big eagle circling the camp.

CHAPTER 4

The morning the plane arrived, Frank and I were out with the day herd. It looked like a big eagle from where we were, circling the camp a couple of times and disappearing behind the buttes. Robbins rode into camp right away and I trailed the horses in.

Hogan landed the Piper Cub on a salt sage flat near the water hole. By the time I got the horses into the corral, they were fueling the plane. Hogan had come from his home in Scottsbluff, Nebraska, and wanted a full tank when he took to the desert.

On his previous trip to Wamsutter, Frank had brought Dave Ally back with him. Dave was about my age, and I welcomed someone to talk to. Dave had helped Frank the summer before and was a good hand with horses.

Frank elected to ride with the pilot on the first attempt at the Chalk Buttes corral. He had seen a wild stallion in the Black Rock Butte area that intrigued him. He described it as a half and half. Dark on the front half and white at the rear. I had seen the same horse the previous spring and had watched for him with no luck since. I had imagined him under my saddle but hadn't had the chance to get a rope on him.

Around 12 Mile Spring, there were several buckskin stallions with harems of mares, prize catches all of them. One young stud, running with several other young studs, was buckskin with four stocking legs up to his knees, a bald face, the dorsal strip and jack-ass stripes behind the knees. I believe he was the most beautiful wild horse I ever saw. These young studs were a fast moving outfit, but the plane would be able to handle them if Hogan could locate them.

Hogan had got a good look at the corral from the air as he circled the camp on his way in. He had noticed the two knolls at the end of the wings of the corral and approved of the general lay of the land.

Excitement was running high as the plane went up for its first attempt at the new corral. Robbins gave last minute instructions to everyone . . . where to be, when to come riding out of hiding. We all anticipated seeing our favorite herd

Robbins, Everette Hogan, and Bert Howard enjoy a smoke and a cup of coffee in the sheep camp.

of wild mustangs come into the trap. They flew northwesterly at first, then began zig-zagging across the desert floor. They were soon out of hearing range, but it was a clear day. We watched as they searched for the bunch of mustangs dominated by that half and half stud. The Piper Cub could cover a lot of ground.

We had turned the day herd out again and grazed them a short distance from the wings of the corral. The hot desert sun beat down on us, and the deer flies and horse flies were bad on the horses. Those deer flies weren't above biting humans, either, so it paid to keep them chased away.

I sat in a small spot of shade provided by my saddle horse, imagining what the corral looked like from the air. It would resemble a huge ring with a 50 yard piece out of it where the opening was. Riding in on the main trail

CHAPTER 4

We used the day herd as decoys.

from the northwest, nothing was visible until you were well into the enclosure of the wings.

After about two hours, the engine of the plane could be heard again. We watched the dust boil up from the parched, dry desert floor and knew they had a big bunch of broom tails headed our way.

We worked the day herd back into the wings of the corral, then took up our positions: Two riders behind each knoll at the ends of the corral wings, one rider staying where he could see the mustangs coming in, yet well out of their view.

The first horse to come out of the dust was the half and half. That beautiful, wild stallion was stretched out at a full gallop, trying to lead his harem safely away from that big bird swooping down upon them. The rest of the herd was strung out for about a mile. We could barely make them out through the cloud of dust. We couldn't even guess how many there might be. The stud tried to circle back towards his home range. The beauty of the Chalk Butte corral was that it was built on a natural getaway for wild horses. Once they were on the strip, it was almost impossible to overtake them on a saddle horse. The softness of the strip made it doubly difficult for a horse carrying a rider.

When the tail end of the wild bunch finally entered the wings, Dad and I rode out, yelling at the top of our voices,

The east wing of the corral leaked horses.

hoping to get the last ones corralled before the first ones turned and came back out. Short and Dave stayed at the wing opening to stop any that might turn back.

As I rode up over the last little hill overlooking the corral, it was apparent that the east wing of the corral had leaked horses. About ten head of horses were out on the Red Strip, running for life itself. They were being led by a beautiful stallion, half white and half dark. He reminded me of a buck antelope as he ran, swiftly and gracefully, to freedom. Although the stallion had gotten away, we ended up with a very successful roundup. Twenty-five wild horses were in the new corral.

We repaired the wing and, the next day, Dad went up in the plane with Hogan. I believe it was Dad's first and only plane ride. He thoroughly enjoyed it and said the most fun was being able to pass any old stud on the desert. The following day the wind came up so I didn't get my plane ride. Quite a disappointment to me then, but, in retrospect, I'm sure glad Dad got to go up on the good day.

Chapter 5

After several days of successful roundup with the plane, we had a good sized herd of wild ones corralled. Frank had made a deal to take them to Rawlins to stage a wild horse rodeo at the fairgrounds there. The show billings were up and tickets were going like hot cakes. All we had to do was show up with enough of the wild ones to put on a real wild west show.

We began trailing the herd eastward from the Chalk Buttes. Our first night was spent at the Red Desert Ranch. It was a real treat to sleep in the bunkhouse there. This part of the desert was all strange to me, and it was a great surprise to see a ranch out in the middle of nowhere. They had a dam across a deep draw to irrigate a little hay crop. It really showed up green in the desert.

Up at daybreak, we got a big breakfast under our belts and soon had the herd out to graze. After a couple of hours in that deep, grassy draw, the horses were ready for the trail again. The road we followed eastward from the Red Desert Ranch wasn't much more than a trail. There were two tracks winding their way between sagebrush and rocks, occasionally detouring around washouts. The old truck bounced along slowly. We almost kept up to it with the horses.

We passed the dugout cabin Frank had built and watered the horses at Flat Spring. Bedded down for the night at the artesian well, we had a first hand experience of how that trap worked. We caught ten head during the night there.

The following night a light mist started to fall as darkness closed in on us. We were at the old stagecoach station, about 25 miles north of Rawlins. Wild Horse Robbins treated us to Dutch oven baking powder biscuits and cowboy beans. The chow tasted wonderful after a long, hard day in the saddle.

We were fortunate for the shelter of the old hotel. We started a fire in the stove to take the chill off and Dave, Short, and I had a quick look around.

The hotel consisted of six rooms. It must have been quite a place in its day. It had been a relay station where the stagecoach changed to fresh horses. There was a good spring of water out back which was probably the main reason for its existence in, what seemed like, no-man's land. This was truly an oasis.

After a good night's sleep on the old hotel floor, we headed the mustangs south. We grazed them frequently because we didn't have far to go on the final leg of our journey. Just after sundown, we corralled them at a little ranch just north of Rawlins, about a mile west of the highway. We took them to the fairgrounds the next day. Fortunately, several people rode out to help us. We needed all the help we could get. Some of the mustangs tried to break away when the first Union Pacific train came whistling through.

Later that evening, the Superior coal miner who had cheated Dad paid a visit to the fairgrounds holding pens, announcing to everyone that he wanted to see if we had any of his horses in the bunch. Frank replied, "You had better take a good look, you SOB, because, when I get done with you, you won't be able to see!" With that, he doubled up his fist, brought it up from the ground, and landed it square on the chin of the coal miner, sending him sprawling. He got to his feet and began fanning the side of his face with his hat, calling for his wife to bring his gun from the pickup. Robbins yelled, "Get your gun, you SOB, and I'll run this pitchfork clear through your guts." As Robbins picked up the fork, nobody doubted his sincerity. The coal miner's truck was seen leaving the fairgrounds shortly after that.

The first day of the rodeo featured saddle bronc riding. Short and I were assigned the job of keeping the broncs in the squeeze pens which kept us plenty busy. When I heard the announcer call Mickey McNight coming out of chute number 3 on a wild gray stallion, I took off long enough to watch.

CHAPTER 5

The first day of the rodeo featured saddle bronc riding.

Mickey was a drifter who worked on various ranches, not spending much time at any one of them. He rode into our camp one time riding a nice looking bay mare. He had to ride her into the corral because she wasn't yet broke to lead. Mick was an artist who specialized in western and rodeo scenes. He could have sold his pictures, but, as far as I know, the only ones he sold were traded in saloons for drinks. I had built up quite an admiration for him. He was a likable guy with a lot of talent.

The gray was a stout, blocky-built horse we had kept in our day herd for about a month. We hadn't tried to break him since he wasn't saddle horse material. He would probably be made a pack horse or light draft horse. He was plenty snaky, though; and I knew Mick was in for a good ride.

As I approached chute 3 from the back side, I heard Mick say, "You take a deep seat, a long rein, and a short ride, turn him out!" The gate swung open, and horse and rider exploded into the arena, each determined to outdo the other. The gray was a strong horse and hit the ground hard. About the third jump, the whole seat ripped out of Mick's Levi's. He made a championship ride until the eight second whistle blew. I'm sure he was relieved to see the pickup man coming his way.

The wild horse rodeo was a big success, with thrills and spills galore. We split up with Robbins after the rodeo as winter was quickly drawing near. Dad traded several horses for a Model A Ford in Rawlins so we didn't have to trail a pack animal. Short and I headed our share of the horses

Most of the rodeo stock was right off the desert.

west, along Highway 30, and Dad followed along with the car. We stayed on the highway for three days, making camp the first night near Creston where we happened on some abandoned corrals for the horses. The next night we put them in the railroad stock pens in Wamsutter. We were treated to a good home-cooked meal at Dave Ally's home. Dave had stayed with Robbins and was helping him take his horses to the Glenrock Ranch, so Mrs. Ally was happy to have us around her table telling stories of her son and the wild horse roundup.

The last night out, we held the horses in a set of sheep corrals north of the Table Rock Station. We were a little unsettled about leaving them in low corrals, but not one of them was out in the morning. From Table Rock, we headed northwest with the horses. We split up here, as Dad had to go to Bitter Creek and then north to stay on the road.

As I approached our camp at 12 Mile, I could see that something was wrong. The tent was in shreds. There hadn't been any high winds, and, besides, wind wouldn't have cut canvas into shreds like this. Dad and I drew our own conclusion about that. It looked to us like the coal miner had gotten in the last lick.

It wasn't long before I was invited to join my brothers, Short, Don, and Chuck in World War II and then the Korean Conflict. That was the end of wild horse adventures for me.

Frank produced 16 of his famous "Robbins Wild Horse Rodeos" which were held annually at the ranch near Glenrock. Most of the stock used was right off the Desert, hand picked for performance by the wild horse king, himself.

During the World War II, the stockmen needed every bit of range grass to feed their cattle and sheep. They got quite concerned about the build-up of mustang herds on the Red Desert. The horse market had been poor and, with the demand down, nobody was running or gathering them. Talk was beginning to circulate among ranchers of exterminating them. Frank got wind of this and attended the next meeting of the grazing association.

Robbins walked in and, in his low, almost drawling, voice said, "I'm heah to represent the hawses." He challenged the

Robbins' wild horses wait for shipment in stock pens at Wamsutter, Wyoming.

wisdom of eliminating the wild horse herds, explaining that a little mustang blood produced a better, more intelligent horse. Frank said he could round them up with an airplane by building blind corrals to trap them in. A deal was made with the grazing association for Wild Horse Robbins to rid the range of the wild horses. Luckily, Frank had the foresight always to leave 50 to 75 head to insure their survival.

The newspapers picked up on the story and many people were offended by the idea of running horses with the mechanized, flying saddle horse. They were led to believe that too many mares were leaving their colts behind and many other wild horses were crippled in the process. Frank wrote a letter to the local newspaper explaining that ranchers paid the government to graze their stock on open range and couldn't be blamed for not wanting it all grazed off by wild horses. Robbins related his experience in rounding up these horses on horseback, a process that crippled many a good saddle horse. He continued:

CHAPTER 5

You've got to keep close behind a herd of wild horses, or the leaders will get away. And the leaders are always the best horses. The little colts get tired and drop out, and the mares seldom go back to look for them after being chased by a rider. The airplane method is more of a hazing proposition. The horses aren't pushed hard. The pilot herds them from quite a distance once he has them headed towards the corral. In this process, colts can keep up with their mothers. When the pilot reaches the wings of the corral, he swoops down on the rear of the herd to crowd them into the corral. The horses don't get as excited and don't run into the sides of the corral, injuring themselves, as much as they do when run by riders.

Toots had, among her keepsakes, a copy of the actual letter in Frank's handwriting.

After reading the article WILD HORSES, AN ASSET OR A LIABILITY, by J. Mayne McArthur in the June issue of Western Horseman, also including other articles regarding the future of the wild horses, I would like to express my views on the subject.

Having spent over 30 years in the business of corralling wild horses in several western states I believe I am qualified to speak in this regard.

The wild horses have been here a long time and, with no one supervising them, they showed no tendency to inbreed where there were many of them. Also, nature did a big part in keeping them from becoming too numerous.

It has been suggested that corralling them by horse back, with no thought of the noble saddle horse that needs to run many miles to do this and is often a failure. Some have suggested selling a license and letting people shoot the older ones out of the herds.

Well, people who like horses do not approve of having these sort of sports in our country. Also, many other horses would be killed or crippled in a plan of that sort.

In other words, there is no way to sort wild horses, only by corralling them. I have corralled upward of 30,000 head in 30 years work and find the most humane method is by airplane, with an experienced pilot. They have to know the art of corralling horses besides having many hours of flying experience.

I believe to supervise the wild horses properly, there should be some stockmen who pay for the grass on Federally controlled land on the advisory board who seldom complain of a few wild horses and would be in a position to determine when there were too many on different ranges.

I am hoping the horses will be given a fair break and not be subject to some plan dreamed up at a desk by a swivel chair expert.

Long live the wild horses.

                Frank Robbins
                P.O. Box One
                Glenrock, Wyo. 82637

P.S. I will quote Mr. McArthur's statement as to the wild colts being weaned in July and August. I have weaned many in October and November and, without hay or grain or both, they will not stand the winter months in most western states.

Robbins watches for his pilot to herd wild horses into a corral. Robbins believed corralling horses by plane to be the most humane method.

CHAPTER 5

The Chain Lakes trap produced a lot of good horses. The most outstanding of all was Buck, one of the traditional roan-buckskin Chain Lakers. The young stallion was caught, broke, trained, and tutored by Wild Horse Robbins. He was such a pretty horse, with such a pleasant disposition that Frank gave him to Toots for her personal mount.

Having been a wild horse, Buck was a thinker, and was always about a jump ahead of any wild ones in their skirmishes. An excellent roping horse, he was never jerked off his feet by any horse, and Robbins had him tied onto some mighty big, mean, old, wild stallions.

Once, Frank had roped a big, wild stud from Buck's back. While he was fighting the stallion, the rest of the bunch was getting out of the corral. Frank jumped off and ran, on foot, to stop them. When he got back, he found Buck, sitting down on his rump like a dog, letting the wild horse, still roped to him, run around and around in the corral.

Another time, Robbins had entered a corral to sort out some mares when a mean stallion charged him on old Buck. Buck just wheeled around, then kicked the wild horse and drove him off.

Buck had his own blanket, a luxury seldom enjoyed by any cow pony. This old boy loved his oats and didn't need to be hobbled to keep him around.

One time, as Robbins and the pilot returned from a trip to town, there stood old Buck, on the only strip of ground suitable to land the airplane for miles around. The old pony knew it was oats time. The plane had to make several passes before he moved off so it could set down.

There is something unexplainable about the way some of those wild horses break out. Once they understand you can handle them and won't hurt them, there comes a kind of understanding between man and horse. They become eager learners and will work their hearts out for you. This is the way it was with Buck and Frank. They became friends for life.

Robbins once said, "Buck can do everything but read and write, and I'm not too sure he can't do that." Buck was retired at the Robbins ranch near Glenrock where he lived, fat and high spirited, to be 36 years old. A little fence

Robbins and Buck.

CHAPTER 5

encircles his grave with a headstone carved by his master's hand. The inscription reads, "Buck, the best horse I ever rode."

Joe Keenan, a Glenrock rancher and friend of the Robbins, tells a story of Frank and Buck. One time, when Frank was in his early 60s, several local cow hands were rounding up a bunch of cattle for the Engleking Brothers. The cattle were wild. Some cows, five years old, had never been branded. Joe was riding a good, little black horse he called Lucky and was pretty well mounted.

When those cattle took off running, they left everybody behind. All except one. Wild Horse Robbins on Buck stayed right with them. The country was rough and hilly, just what old Buck was used to. They finally got them into the Burlington Railroad stockyards where they could work them.

Frank roped one of the big, unbranded cows. When she hit the end of the rope, she was sideways to old Buck. Buck would never have let this happen if it hadn't been for a pile of loose gravel left by a construction crew. Halfway across the gravel, Buck couldn't get facing the old cow and was pulled down. It all happened so fast, Robbins went down with him, striking his head on the ground with a thud.

Everyone thought old Frank was a goner. After about 15 minutes, he staggered to his feet, limping on his bad leg. His eyes seemed to look in separate directions; but finally he said in almost a whisper, "I think we had better put two ropes on them."

When the steers were finally loaded into rail cars and the days work was done, Joe casually remarked, "You've had kind of a rough day today, haven't you, Frank?" Frank answered, just as casually, "Oh, about ordinary." To a guy as tough as Wild Horse Robbins, it was, perhaps, an ordinary day.

Joe also tells of another time in the late 1930s when Glenrock held a community picnic in the city park. An old guy was leading a big, bay mare around, snubbed to his saddle horn, and bragging that nobody could ride her. Nobody seemed to want to try, either. Finally, Frank walked over to the old cowboy and, in his low voice, said, "I'll ride your horse if you really want her rode." His brother, Doc, eared her down right there in the city park. Frank threw his saddle on her and cinched it down tight, stepping aboard. At the command, "Turn her loose," the old mare bogged her old head, humped up her back, and gave her best shot at bucking Frank off. There were no pickup men or hazers, nobody to help, just Robbins and that bucking, squealing, bawling old mare. When she finally quit bucking, Frank got off. That old cowboy was really steamed that somebody rode his horse.

The life that Wild Horse Robbins led was hard on his anatomy. Toots figured he had, at some time or another, broken every bone in his body.

One day, while trying out a new horse, he decided to see if gunfire would spook the old pony. He fired the pistol and the horse leaped into the air. The next shot went right through Frank's finger. The finger healed well, just leaving a small bump.

His left hand was minus two fingers from a roping accident when Frank was moving a mustang from the corral to the pasture. The mustang took off after the loop was dropped on his neck. When the horse hit the end of the rope, Frank's two fingers were in a kink in the lariat. One was neatly amputated. The other was just dangling, so Frank took his own knife and finished the job. He wrapped his handkerchief around the stub, put his glove on, and took the stallion to pasture, He eventually saw the doctor for it, but he wasn't much for going to doctors. They always wanted to hospitalize him. He just didn't have time to be laid up.

Robbins always maintained he would rather die with his boots on, doing battle with a good horse. He almost met his maker in the form of a big black stallion. They had corralled this stud the year before, but he jumped over a 15 foot corral fence to freedom. The plane successfully brought him back to a new corral the following summer, and he was corralled for keeps. Frank went into the corral to load the wild ones into a truck. Without warning, the black stallion attacked him on his saddle horse, breaking Frank's leg in two places. He escaped by crawling under the fence. Robbins said he was a beautiful horse, but he kept biting and kicking the plank corral. He finally ran into the solid corral wall and killed himself. When the horse attacked with his ears laid back and teeth showing, Frank noted his teeth indicated he was 30 years old.

After the long journey to Rock Springs in the back of a station wagon, over more than 100 miles of bumpy roads, the wild horse king was ready for the hospital this time. He stayed the shortest time possible to mend a broken leg. When he was ready to leave, the nurses offered to help him out. He said, "If I can't make it on my own, I'll stay awhile longer." He hobbled around Rock Springs a few days, but soon returned to the desert to take up the chase again. It could very well have been while he was hospitalized that he wrote these poems.

THE RENEGADE STALLION

> A jaded renegade stallion
> Stood high on the top of a hill.
> All his comrades had vanished
> Since the "Taylor Bill."
> One by one they'd died
> Till he was left all alone.
> Died from ranger's bullets
> And the coyotes polished their bones.
> Many's the time he'd dodged them
> And once was wounded quite bad.
> He stood for days in a hollow
> His plans for the future were sad.
> Anyway, the horse chasers had left there
> And drifted to parts unknown.
> Then there was the report of a rifle
> And the coyotes polished his bones.
> So it's farewell to the wide open spaces,
> You've driven us from them at last.
> We wish you success in the future,
> With an abundance of water and grass.

ROBBINS RED DESERT

I've lived all my life in a saddle
All I know is to rope an old cow.
I've never worked on a sheep ranch,
And damned if I'll follow a plow.

Toots found this last poem written on a small piece of paper among his keepsakes a short while after his death. He had never shown it to her.

THAT OLD A-FORK SADDLE TREE

Layin' out by the round corral
Is a thing they call a saddle.
It's seen a lot of hardships
And been through many a battle.
The skirts are dried and wrinkled,
And the stamping is no longer there.
The horn has seen a million dallies,
And the steel in the center is bare.

But it stays on a horse where you set it,
The stirrups hang where they should be.
The riggin' rings are long and narrow,
On this old A Fork saddle tree.
And when I get aboard one.
He will know he's inhabited, too.
For the ones that have bucked me out of it
Were tough ones, and only a few.

The following article was also written by Frank. WHAT A HORSE is about a horse raised on the Robbins' Ranch, a cross between a Hamiltonian sire and a mustang dam.

WHAT A HORSE

Pictured is Buddy, Hamiltonian bred, dark bay gelding, raised at Robbins Ranch, Glenrock, Wyo.

Buddy was born May 1940 and was killed June 1973 by lightening, age 33 years, 1 month.

He was broken to hackamore when 5 years old and to Spanish bit at 7 years old. He weighted 1130 pounds in working condition. He was used to run wild horses in Wyoming and Nevada

CHAPTER 5

for four years and outran and corralled many wild bunches for the other 10 years he was used to corral wild horses as they were brought in by airplane during which time over thirty thousand head were corralled, so I believe he held a record that will never be surpassed. Buddy was never off his feet in all this work, nor was he ever jerked down by roping and many wild horses were roped off him. He was never wind buffed nor lamed in any way, nor did he ever have a sore back.

In later years, when I built a hunting lodge, Buddy drug enough house logs off a steep mountain to build the lodge, 40 by 60 feet, along with enough corral poles to build many corrals. He drug these by the saddle horn.

He was then used in the hunting camp. Buddy was a good walker, a real trotter and could run a hole in the air if need be.

He spent his last 5 years on our ranch in the hay meadows. Due to loosing all his teeth, we fed him ground hay and grain for the balance of his life.

The accompanying photo was taken about a month before his death and he is buried beneath the cottonwood tree behind him. I hope this picture and history serves to tell people what a good horse can do for his owner in a life time.

Frank Robbins
P.O. Box One
Glenrock, Wyo. 82637

Robbins and Buddy. "What a horse."

Chapter 6

During the years of rounding up wild horses, Frank and Toots would occasionally take a bit of leisure time. They enjoyed hunting Indian artifacts such as arrowheads, spearheads, stone hammerheads, and anything of this nature they could find. The area around Sand Lake was a good place to pick up these articles. The Indians preferred sandy ground to camp on. I'm sure the lakes among the sand dunes were always a good place for the Indians to hunt as well as a good source of water for camp use.

Finding Indian artifacts requires a sharp eye and some "know how" about Indian life. Most of the chips and flint will be found near an old camp site. Fire rocks, which have been used in campfires, will usually spark the interest of anyone with knowledge of artifacts. Although scattered, the rocks still show signs of having been burned. They were used for cooking, heating, and, probably, for the heating of flint so Indian craftsmen could chip it into tools. Their skilled hands made very small and sharp points for killing birds and small game. Larger arrowheads were made for killing deer, antelope, and other big game.

Many spearheads have been found and were probably used, primarily, for killing buffalo. Heavy stone hammerheads were used in tool making, stake driving, much the same as steel hammers are used in our own culture.

Many of the hard rocks like red flint, obsidian, and sugar rock were mined and used to trade for hides, food, and other supplies needed by the tribes. Sugar rock was mined in eastern Wyoming, near Lusk. Some of the rocks had been hauled from as far away as Oregon and Montana.

The Robbins' collection is housed in the museum in Douglas, Wyoming.

"Frank, we're almost out of meat," called Toots from the door of the camp as Robbins was riding off to oversee another wild horse roundup. It was a warm day on the desert, and she knew he wouldn't hunt for an antelope or deer before late afternoon or evening. There was, however, a good chance she wouldn't see him again before dark.

Frank instinctively reached his right hand down to his saddle scabbard to make certain his trusty 30-30 rifle was there. The old gun was his constant companion, but he had been known to leave it in camp.

From the high knoll where he waited for the plane to bring the mustangs, he had a view of a wide area of the countryside. This enabled him to see several herds of antelope. Antelope far outnumbered deer on the desert, so it would be the most likely game he would bring in for camp meat.

The pilot had thrown several bunches of horses together, and they were kicking up a lot of dust. Robbins used the time waiting for the horses to come in to survey the area in the opposite direction of the horses for a nice buck. He hoped it would be a young, fat one that would be tender and tasty. If he spotted one in this area, chances were less of the horses spooking them out. After the horse running was over, Wild Horse Robbins would go hunting.

The drone of the aircraft engine grew loud and steady. Frank quickly diverted his attention to the herd coming in. The experienced pilot had them headed right for the trap. As Frank watched, crouched down behind the knoll out of sight, the lead horses sped past. Soon the whole herd was in the wings of the corral.

Robbins mounted old Buck as the rider at the end of the other wing mounted his horse. Together they followed the thundering herd, engulfed in a cloud of dust, to the trap, quickly closing the gate before the horses had time to come back out.

Frank told the other wrangler to go to camp for supper. He was going hunting for some camp meat. With that, he rode off in the direction of the herds he had watched earlier.

It was nearing sundown as he left the corral. He knew he would need a lot of luck to get an antelope before dark.

CHAPTER 6

This was the best time of day to hunt, though. Especially since antelope were out of season. There would be less chance of being caught in the act. Game wardens were seldom seen in this remote area in those days, but there was always a chance of one showing up when you least expected him.

Letting old Buck pick his way among the sagebrush and rocks, he traveled in the general direction of his prey. The sun had disappeared below the horizon and the cooling air felt good to the rugged, weather-beaten mustanger. Earlier, he had spotted a place where a little draw made a bend. He decided to hide just beyond that, behind a little knoll. After tying old Buck to a big sage brush in the bottom of the draw, he removed the 30-30 from its scabbard and proceeded on foot to locate the herd. As he approached the crest of the hill, he walked slowly and carefully so as not to spook any game. Taking off his ten-gallon hat, he peeked over the small hill to see a bunch of 10 or 12 antelope with a very respectful looking buck in charge. Too far away for a good shot, he cautiously made his way back to Buck and rode a little farther down the draw. When he reached a place close enough, he again left his horse and traveled on foot. This time, he peeked over the ridge, he put the buck in his sights and downed him with the first shot. He was a nice young buck with plenty of size to him. As Frank field dressed him, the tallow on the guts indicated some very fine meals of antelope meat in camp.

After replacing the gun in the scabbard, Robbins led Buck over to the antelope. Many horses throw a fit when they smell blood and want nothing to do with transporting the smelly mess, but old Buck, a veteran of many hunting trips, took the whole thing calmly. Frank soon had the antelope draped over his saddle and took off, leading his burdened horse towards the wild horse camp.

It was dark when Frank led Buck into camp. He hung the antelope on one of the tallest corral posts and headed for his supper before skinning it. The cool air would cool it thoroughly overnight.

Robbins was up at daybreak to take care of the meat. It felt really cool to the touch and was in good shape to be quartered and placed in meat sacks. By the time he had it quartered, the other hands were up. The meat was placed on the shady side of the camp wagon under their bedrolls. The bedrolls would act as insulation, protecting against the oncoming heat of the day. The hide and remains were disposed of in a washout far enough from camp so the odor wouldn't find its way back.

The day went along as usual. Frank, the pilot, and the other wranglers went out to round up horses. Toots stayed in camp to take care of the cooking. She hadn't banked 100% on the success of Frank's hunt so, the night before, had put on a pot of beans to soak and parboiled a chunk of salt pork to remove some of the salt from it. About midmorning, she put the beans and pork into a Dutch oven and set it on a hot bed of coals. This typical roundup style meal would be ready for supper.

As the evening shadows grew longer, the sun appeared to snuggle in between Steamboat Mountain and the Tables as it made its way towards the horizon. The plane touched down on the salt sage flat and rattled to a stop in a cloud of dust. About the same time, a long streak of dust appeared, rising above the old road leading in from the east. The camp was close enough to the road to be plainly visible to anyone passing by. Out in this remote area, anyone traveling would be certain to stop for awhile.

By the time the pickup truck rolled to a stop, it was plain to see the visitor was the Sweetwater County game warden. This created a little excitement in camp. No one acted nervous, though, or let on like there was any anxiety.

Frank invited him to stay for supper with true western hospitality. The warden readily accepted the invitation. Now western hospitality didn't include a table and chairs. Wranglers were expected to find their own place to sit and eat their meal. The warden filled his plate with beans and biscuits, filled his coffee cup and, wouldn't you know it, headed right for the bedrolls and sat right down on a corner of the pile.

There were some tense moments as he visited about horse roundups and asked questions about various species of game spotted from the air by the pilot. After he finished eating,

CHAPTER 6

he got up, thanked the Robbins for the meal and drove away into the night. Everyone breathed a sigh of relief and had a good laugh before turning in for a good night's sleep.

Frank turned in, too, but lay awake, mentally reviewing the events of his busy day. He wondered what the warden would have said or done if he had discovered the illegal game in his camp. His mind drifted back to another time in one of his earlier camps, before they had started to use the airplane.

Frank had returned to camp about dusk, riding a tired horse who had run with a fast bunch of mustangs for 30 miles before losing them. He was tired and, by no means pleased, to find a game warden waiting in camp. This was a man Frank had known for years and considered a friend. Frank invited him to stay for supper, as he would have done for anyone at that time of day. This warden had also accepted the invitation.

After a hearty supper, the warden casually announced, "Frank, I'll have to take you in. There are sage chicken bones and feathers, antelope bones, and plenty of evidence that you have been eating wild game." Wild Horse Robbins was enraged. This guy had taken advantage of his hospitality and friendship. Now, he was hoping to put a feather in his cap by arresting him. Frank reached up above the door, removed the 30-30 from its pegs, levered the action to throw a live round of ammunition into the firing chamber, all in one move, and uttered, "Now, you SOB, you had better get out of here while you still can."

The guy probably didn't expect this to happen, but, knowing Robbins as well as he did, lost no time in making his departure ... never to call again.

After running horses all day, everybody, including the pilot, had worked up a good appetite. Supper was always a good meal; and everyone took on a good fill, moving a little closer to the campfire as the meal progressed. The desert really cools off when the sun goes down. As darkness settles in, the warmth of the fire feels good. Then, too, everybody was jockeying for position for story time.

Just as soon as Frank finished eating, he took out his old pipe, hit it against the hard heel of his boot to knock the ashes loose, and filled it with new tobacco. Everyone watched in anticipation, knowing he would light it, lean back against his old saddle, and, when he was as comfortable as he could get, begin to spin yarns about his adventures. And his whole life had been one big adventure. He told one about roping horses at night after they had filled up on water.

He took after a big horse, a beauty. After chasing him for about eight miles, he finally got his rope on it, but couldn't drag him into the corral. He finally resorted to hobbling the wild horse and then hit the sack for some much needed rest. Next morning he was eager to see what kind of horse he had caught. He found a beautiful chestnut with a big, bald face . . . and, someone else's brand on his hip.

Another time, when roping a stallion, he jumped from his horse and the rein broke. Both horses ran off, leaving Frank about fifteen miles from water with a blazing sun overhead. The horse hadn't been trained to stand still when he had something on the rope, so he just trotted along with the stud. The rope must have been choking the stallion some, because, every once in awhile, he stopped to rest. Just about the time Wild Horse Robbins got near his saddle horse, they would take off on the trot again. He finally circled them and headed them down a trail towards camp. He knew, if they stayed on the trail, they would have to cross a draw. He figured his horse would get his front leg over the rope when he stepped across the draw, then would be afraid of getting tangled up and would stand still. It happened just that way. The very next order of business, after returning to camp, was to train that horse to stand when he had something on the end of the rope.

One day, Frank and his crew corralled a big buckskin stallion by plane. When they walked up for a look, he jumped over a ten foot corral from a flat-footed start, and got away. Years later, in early spring, after a hard winter, he was spotted again tending a nice herd of mares. He was terribly thin. The mares herded easily, but he was reluctant, remembering the corral. He finally decided to follow the mares and trotted

CHAPTER 6

Mare and colt. The mares herded easily.

into the trap. He headed right for the same spot where he had jumped out before. No luck for the old horse this time. He was too old to make the jump. Realizing this horse's days were limited, Frank opened the gate and sent him on his way to freedom.

Frank claimed the wildest horse he ever captured was a black stallion with stocking feet. No one ever rode him although many tried. One year, when the officials for the Casper rodeo asked for a real bad horse, Robbins took the black along. Frank offered to put his halter on, but the officials said their chute crew would handle that little detail. When they tried, the old horse grabbed that halter in his teeth, bit it in two, threw it down and stomped on it, and then began biting kindling sized splinters out of the chute. The Casper rodeo officials never repeated their request.

Of course, all wild horses aren't so fierce. Frank sold a black horse to a fellow who intended to train him to do trick work in rodeos. The horse was doing real well, except, after a few days, he ran away. The following year, Robbins caught the same horse who had, somehow, traveled nearly 400 miles back to his home, the Red Desert. Mustangs have a strong homing instinct. Even though they may be trucked at night, over winding highways, they have an uncanny ability to find their way back to their home range.

Frank also told an old story about a buffalo chase. Sometime around 1920, Governor Carey owned and operated the famous CY ranches east of Glenrock (now the Bixby Ranch). He imported quite a herd of buffalo and turned them into his pastures adjoining the ranch. They were quite wild and stayed as far from the buildings as possible. Frank and his brother, Harry, decided to rope some of them. Having pretty good saddle horses, they proceeded to outrun the bunch. They soon discovered, however, the buffalo had speed to spare. They headed them toward a high bank an Boxelder Creek, the main bank being at least 30 feet high, figuring this would slow them up some. To the boys' surprise, the buffalo went over the bank at full speed and landed below, still running. Frank's and Harry's planning went to the buffalo's advantage.

The Piper Cub proved to be the most successful airplane for running horses. It had the lowest stalling speed and the most maneuverability. During the filming of the fighting stallions the Piper Aircraft Company donated the use of a Piper Cub to be used for the wild horse roundup. Mr. William Piper was so enthused about the venture that he paid the wild horse wranglers an unexpected visit on the desert. Mr. Piper was thrilled to see his plane, piloted by Roy Lamoreau, corral a herd of wild mustangs shortly after his arrival.

The Robbins camp was visited by many notables over the years. Among them were Ken Curtis, better known as

CHAPTER 6

A herd of wild mustangs is corralled by plane. Note the wings of the corral hidden in the draw, camouflaged with brush.

Festus Haggen on the GUNSMOKE series, and Mr. and Mrs. Arthur Lake. Arthur was famous for playing Dagwood on the BLONDIE series.

The pilots of the airborne mechanized saddle horses were many, each one a professional. Wild horse running was no place for a beginner or inexperienced pilot. When flying close to the ground and making tight turns, there is no room for error. Included among the fliers were Everett Hogan, Clyde Ice, Howard Schrum, Roy Lamoreau, Walt Williams, and Curley Wetzel. They all deserve a lot of credit for the success of the Robbins Wild Horse roundups.

My Dad spoke often of Clyde Ice, who he admired as both a pilot and coyote hunter. Dad used hounds when hunting coyotes and could often get two or three a day, but Clyde Ice could get that many in 10 or 15 minutes, shooting them from the plane. Dad recommended Clyde to Robbins when we were at the Chalk Buttes. He told Frank he would be good at running horses because of his coyote hunting experience.

Clyde Ice and Robbins study an area map. Note Model D car in background.

When I met this man on his ranch near Spearfish, South Dakota, he had passed the 90 year mark by six or seven years. When I inquired about his health he said, "I'm doing real good, except my landing gear is giving out on me."

Clyde grew up on a farm near Miller, South Dakota. He traded two used cars for his first airplane, a World War I biplane, and taught himself to fly in a wheat field. "Just figured the gol durned thing out and flew it." He began hauling passengers the next day. He went to Detroit and helped assemble the first tri-motor Ford sold for commercial transportation, then took it barnstorming to many of the major cities in the country. He thought he knew quite a lot about horses, but said, "Those Red Desert mustangs gave me quite an education." Clyde said he really enjoyed the time he spent flying for Wild Horse Robbins.

He had installed a more powerful engine in his Piper Club to make it more maneuverable. Horse running required much

CHAPTER 6

steep banking and sudden pull-ups while flying dangerously close to the ground. He had also installed a wing tank for an added supply of gasoline to satisfy the thirst of the bigger engine.

It was only after Clyde took her into a steep bank in a narrow canyon while trying to turn a herd of mustangs that he found out the installation was wrong. The engine sputtered and stopped. He knew what the trouble was. He had the end of the tank with the outlet too high and no gas flowed to the engine.

Flying low in the canyon, he had no choice but to force land his plane. Nothing was damaged, but the plane had to be dismantled and carried out of the canyon by manpower.

On one of his trips to Wamsutter, Frank was asked how his wild horse roundup was coming. The reply came, "We're at a standstill right now. That daredevil pilot got too close to an old stud and got the propeller caught in his tail. When that old horse runs down and we get the plane back, we'll go at it again."

Chapter 7

During World War II, the market for horses increased nationally and even expanded to overseas markets.

Frank continued to round up mustangs on the Red Desert until they had been thinned out sufficiently on the north side of the Union Pacific Railroad. He had heard about a place called Dobe Town, south of the railroad, so he made several scouting trips to that area. The country around Dobe Town was nothing more than a bunch of clay formations which resembled a small town when viewed from a distance. The terrain to the south was much rougher than the desert Frank had been occupying.

Centuries of erosion by wind and water had cut deep canyons into the clay soil and sand rock. Robbins searched for and found a blind canyon for the site of his corral. The canyon had three sides which were straight up, ranging in height from 20 to 50 feet. By fencing off the entrance and putting a wide gate across it, he would have a perfect corral. He had to fence off a couple other canyons to keep the mustangs running in the right direction.

During one of his trips to town for supplies, he heard of a wild palomino stallion running in the Dobe Town country. Several wild horse outfits had been after him, but he had managed to give them the slip.

Frank saw this as a challenge. His pilot, Walt Williams, was instructed to find the golden horse and bring him in. This airplane jockey knew his business. About two hours later, he returned with the beautiful stallion and 13 head of mares and colts. The stud was perfect in every way except for the fact that both ears were cropped, probably frozen off in a winter storm when he was a colt.

The stallion looked at his captors in defiance, completely circling the corral several times and trying to scale the 20 foot embankment. He found no way out.

Frank knew he had a prize catch. This beautiful, golden palomino, with flowing mane and tail and four white stocking feet, had almost perfect quarter horse conformation. Frank also knew he would have a fight on his hands when he roped him.

After much squealing, snorting, kicking, and biting at the rope, the horse was finally thrown down. They haltered him, but the beautiful coat was never marked with a branding iron.

Frank figured he was probably a descendant of a very fine palomino quarter horse that used to range in the Dobe Town area of the desert. Palominos in the wild were unheard of. This could very well be the only one ever captured. The horse, named Desert Dust, was given special treatment. Frank trucked him to the ranch at Glenrock where a half-hearted attempt was made to break him. He fought Robbins all the way. He'd bite the saddle after bucking it off, never surrendering to the experienced hand that had tamed so many wild ones.

Frank decided he was a horse that wasn't supposed to be broke, so he turned him to the pasture with the choice Red Dessert mares he had been hand picking over the years. He sired 19 perfect palomino colts on the Robbins ranch.

The word of the capture of the beautiful stallion soon spread and people came from all around to get a glimpse of him. He was a proud horse and seemed to know when he was on display. He would strut his stuff and really put on a show when a lot of people were around.

Soon there were newspaper reporters, free lance photographers, and Hollywood movie producers gathering photos and information about Desert Dust, the wild stallion. His picture appeared on post cards, billboards and cafe menus just to name a few. He was featured in a Universal Studios short film, FIGHT OF THE WILD STALLIONS, which was nominated for an Academy Award. The film shows Desert

CHAPTER 7

Desert Dust was a horse that wasn't supposed to be broke.

Dust fighting a black, wild stallion that Robbins had just caught. The stallions fought over a harem of mares in a natural setting on the desert.

The Robbins rodeo at Glenrock was also the setting for one of the BLONDIE series episodes entitled, FLYING LADY. This movie featured the famous Desert Dust in the rodeo portion of the show.

FIGHT OF THE WILD STALLIONS featuring Desert Dust was filmed in 1946 on the Red Desert during Frank Robbins' annual wild horse roundup. Universal Studios picked Roy Edwards as director of photography for the project. Prior to this, Roy had specialized in news and news features. Assisted by Jean DuBois, a roving newsreel cameraman from Denver, the two camped on the desert with Robbins and his wranglers, slept in bedrolls, and ate from the chuck wagon.

A limited budget made it impossible to stage the entire event for the camera, so it was worked right in with everyday occurrences as they happened. Cameras and equipment were hauled in light trucks when possible. Where the terrain was too rough, pack horses were used. When the going got even rougher, the cameramen packed the expensive equipment on their own backs.

Everything had to be hidden and downwind of where the wild horses would be running as they approached the corral. Additionally, this all had to be worked into Robbins' everyday roundup. At times, the cameramen thought Frank was picky, but he explained that the slightest sound, movement, or scent of man would be sure to turn the horses back. Frank couldn't afford to lose a herd because some cameraman was in the wrong place.

Once they had the equipment in place and were ready, there was a several hour wait for the plane to bring in the horses. They had agreed to film on Frank's terms, though, so grudgingly cooperated with this gnarly, old cowboy. When the many reels of action-packed film were in the can, Edwards and DuBois knew they had Frank and his persistence to thank for their success.

CHAPTER 7

Some days they were near the trap as they waited. Here they got some shots as a wrangler mounted his steed and put spurs to his horse in hot pursuit of the mustangs.

Sometimes, the camera was placed behind a rock in the trail where the horses stampeded, giving the audience the effect of being run over by a herd of stampeding horses. The dust got so thick as the horses stampeded down the trail that some of them were blinded and lunged into the rock, upsetting the camera. The cameraman barely escaped by leaping behind a huge boulder.

To shoot some of the scenes involving many horses, a little staging was required. The wranglers waited until a couple hundred head had been gathered and then handled until they were somewhat used to being herded. Then scenes were acted out with the big herd. The wranglers stampeded them through fences, and they attempted to climb the steep canyon walls while being filmed by Jean DuBois.

A telephone pole was erected at the edge of the corral for filming the rodeo and corral shots. Spikes were driven into the pole so the cameraman could climb to the top for some spectacular action shots.

They even rigged up a camera on a pack saddle which they tried on a gentle horse until the angle and setting were just right. Then, a wild horse was roped and thrown, and the contraption was put on it. When the wild horse got up and started to buck, it gave the effect of what it looks like through the eyes of a bronc rider.

Some excellent scenes were shot from the plane. The camera was planted in the leading edge of the wing, just above the pilot's head. The camera was fixed in a bracket to photograph the ground ahead of the plane. A cameraman sitting in the seat behind the pilot could easily turn it on and off.

Roy Lamoreau was flying for Robbins during the filming. Up at 3:30 a.m., in the air by daylight, he had a busy schedule, but loved every thrill-packed moment of it.

Roy was raised on a Montana ranch. One of the filming crew remarked, "Whenever we saw Roy, he was either eating, flying, roping, or sleeping."

Making tough flights was part of Roy's business. He had made flights in all kinds of weather, rescuing people who were snowed in, or sick, or crippled. He usually had to land out in the middle of nowhere with not much to land on. Flying of this kind takes real skill and nerves of steel. Robbins used to say, "Roy is half Indian, half horse, and half eagle. This is certainly too many halves, but that is what it takes to corral wild horses."

In preparation for the stallion fight, a newly captured wild stallion was taken away from his harem of mares. Desert Dust was turned with the mares for about two weeks. This set the stage for the fierce battle that ensued. The herd was herded into a narrow, steep canyon where they could be held close enough to the well-positioned cameramen.

When the stallions were turned loose, a terrific battle began. Lunging, rearing, biting, and kicking, each stallion

Robbins turned the beautiful Desert Dust to pasture.

CHAPTER 7

tried to beat the other. This was a thrilling climax to a movie already packed with thrills and spills.

It took about six weeks to film THE FIGHT OF THE WILD STALLIONS, and, of the 50,000 feet of film exposed, only 2,000 was in the finished production. That's show biz!

Ken Curtis, better known as Festus on the popular TV series GUNSMOKE, hired on with Robbins as a wrangler one summer. His ever-present sense of humor made him very popular with Frank and anyone else who happened to come in contact with him.

He remarked that the knowledge of cowboying and the ways of the old west under the tutelage of Wild Horse Robbins was a major asset to his highly successful career as a western actor. The tuition paid in sweat and hard work came a little hard at the time, but it was well worth it.

Toots wasn't at the camp during his stay, so he wasn't favored by her home-cooked meals, but old Frank was no slouch when it came to cooking, so he had nothing to complain about. Frank's baking powder biscuits, baked in a Dutch oven, were fit for a king. Years later, Curtis sent the following letter to Frank.

Mar. 10, 1972

Dear friend Frank,

It sure was good to hear from you after all these years — sure wish I could go back out to the old camp with you again — I'll never forget the great times we had on our wild horse roundup. It's hard to believe that was over 20 years ago. If I'd of had my mule then, we might have corralled a helluva lot more mustangs.

Don't get confused when you look at this picture — *I'm the one wearin' the hat!!*

Best regards
your friend
"Festus"
Ken Curtis

Wild Horse Robbins had been invited to New York so Frank could appear on the WE THE PEOPLE radio program. The flight to New York in March of 1946 was a great

Festus.

CHAPTER 7

experience for Frank and Toots. They flew in Roy Lamoreau's Cessna.

The sagebrush-covered hills of Wyoming soon gave way to grassy plains. Then came the patchwork of grain fields as they passed over farm land. They noticed much smoke and haze as they passed over the industrial cities of Pennsylvania, a real change from the clear blue Wyoming skies. Walking the streets of New York in their western attire brought many stares from the New Yorkers and questions from many people asking if they were from Texas. Frank always acted insulted at this query and replied, "No, we are from Glenrock, Wyoming and my horse corral is just south of town." Lamoreau, a rancher pilot, decided to get himself a cap after being questioned about being from the Lone Star state several times. It would have taken more than caps, though, to disguise these trail-worn Red Desert horse runners.

The radio program had a question and answer format. After Don Bolton, the announcer, fielded the numerous questions, Frank explained a wild horse roundup by plane in Wyoming's Red Desert.

The sponsors of WE THE PEOPLE treated Frank, Toots, and Roy to a tour of the city. They really enjoyed their visit, but left with no desire to live in the city made up of tall buildings, heavy traffic, loud noises, and endless streams of people.

On the way home, they stopped in St. Louis for a visit with relatives. Upon returning to Wyoming, though, their thoughts soon returned to the Red Desert and the challenges of the mustangs.

Wamsutter, Wyoming, was the nearest source of supplies for Frank's wild horse operation. This little town was located on the Union Pacific Railroad and Highway 30. Dave Ally lived there with his family. Dave had been one of Robbins' hands on many a roundup. Another young man befriended by Frank was a young upshot named John Bugas. John's family had moved to Wamsutter from Rock Springs, and his father was a construction contractor. Young Bugas was a dependable hand, and Frank and he kept up their friendship long after John went to work for the Ford Motor Company. John climbed the ladder of success in the complex Ford Company to become Henry Ford II's closest confidant.

One story claims that on one of Bugas' visits back to Wyoming, he mentioned to Robbins a new car they were developing at the factory that was small sized, a tough little devil, with a lot of snap and speed. They just hadn't come up with a name, yet, to fit the machine. Robbins commented, "A tough little devil, with a lot of snap and speed sounds just like a mustang. Name it Mustang." That was in the early 60s. The mustang emblem displayed on the little Ford could well have been fashioned from a picture of a wild mustang from the Robbins collection.

Frank was later made an honorary member of the Casper Mustang Club and was taken to Indianapolis to the National Council on Mustang Clubs during the Indy 500 time trials. While in Indianapolis, the club showed the film THE FIGHT OF THE WILD STALLIONS which starred Desert Dust, the wild palomino stallion captured by Wild Horse Robbins on the Red Desert.

Winter on the Red Desert can bring bright sunshine and calm winds, or it can bring low, dark clouds, dropping knee deep snow, whipped up by gale force winds. You don't necessarily have to change days to have both.

The day began bright and shiny, appearing to be a perfect day to drive into Wamsutter to stock up on grub and other supplies. The Robbins were out of oats for the saddle horses and needed kerosene for the lamp. They had resorted to burning a "bitch" for light in camp. Burning a bitch was quite common in the remote areas of the old west. A bitch consisted of waste cooking fat in an open tin can. A piece of cloth, tightly rolled into a wick, would be put down in the oil. After soaking for about an hour, it could be lit with a match to give off light, like a lamp without a chimney. Of course, it flickered and smoked a lot when it was placed in a draft. Additionally, the aroma in the cabin would reflect

CHAPTER 7

whatever had been cooked in the grease. Bacon grease smelled like breakfast all night long.

    The Robbins enjoyed their trips to town. They didn't go often; and, when they did, they visited the folks who ran the Wamsutter Hotel, the Sam Ally family, and many other friends. By the time their visiting was done that day, the sky was clouded over; and the wind was beginning to blow. Wild Horse Robbins didn't like the looks of it. He knew they had to get back to the wild horse camp because he had horses in the corral that needed to be fed and watered. The clouds were low and rolling with increasing wind as they hurried to purchase and load their supplies into the pickup truck.

    The temperature dropped steadily. Snow began falling as they drove out of Wamsutter to return to camp, about 30 miles away. Frank reassured Toots, "If we hurry, we will make it before the snow gets too deep to drive in." Neither spoke much as the truck slowly bounced along the road. They were both worried. They were well aware of the danger they would be in if this developed into a genuine old-fashioned Red Desert blizzard.

    As the snow got deeper, the wheels began to spin, slowing them almost to a standstill. The seasoned rancher hated to stop, knowing darkness would soon be upon them. He soon got out, though, to put the chains on. They breathed easier as they continued to wend their way slowly to their camp. The chains were giving the traction they needed. All of a sudden, the truck started to cough and sputter. Frank talked nice to it, babied it, and, finally, cussed it when it died about two miles from camp. It was froze up. He tried to restart the engine, but the battery was down. Then, he hand-cranked until he was blue in the face and finally gave up to the fact that they would have to walk the rest of the way.

    They were dressed warmly, with overshoes, heavy gloves and warm caps. Seasoned ranchers never get caught unprepared when cold weather is imminent. Darkness closed in around them as they pushed their way into the storm. The wind drove the sleet and snow, stinging their faces;

and Toots had to stop a couple of times to get her vision cleared. Frank, afraid of losing her, took her by the hand to guide her. Blinded by the snow, wind, and darkness, Robbins got off the road. As soon as he realized this, he decided just to keep on walking straight. If he circled to find the road, he knew he would be in danger of losing all sense of direction. They kept plowing through snow and sagebrush. Toots knew they were lost, but wouldn't give up. If they perished, they would go together.

Frank didn't say much, just, once in awhile, a reassuring, "C'mon Toots, we'll make it." She wasn't so sure, but she had a lot of faith in that long, lean cowboy she had married. She was tired and cold. Progress had slowed to almost nothing, and she was about to lie down when they heard a horse whinny. What a joyful sound that was. It was old Buck in camp, wanting his oats.

After a bit of stumbling around, searching for the camp wagon, they finally found it and got inside. Frank soon had a roaring fire in the stove. As they thawed themselves by the fire, Toots had a warm and thankful feeling inside. She figured old Frank must have been blessed with a built-in compass.

Robbins kept the best wild roan and buckskin mares for breeding stock.

CHAPTER 7

Wild Horse Robbins continually strived to improve the wild horse strain. He favored the Chain Lakers and hauled the best roan and buckskin mares home to the ranch.

He had pasture for 400 head and, by the time he decided to slow down a bit and quit rounding up mustangs, he had most of a pasture full.

He developed a breed called Robbins Roans by purchasing full blood quarter horse stallions and turning them with the roan mares.

Throughout his lifetime, Wild Horse Robbins built wild horse corrals in many different states. Wherever there were wild horses, Robbins was after them. His idea for using an airplane proved to be the best way to round up the mustangs.

As Robbins grew older, so grew the aches and pains he had received over the years. He eventually had to sell most of the horses, but always kept a few head down behind the corrals along Deer Creek. He'd proudly show them to visitors, explaining the mother was a mustang from the Red Desert and the father, a papered quarter horse.

Over the years, Robbins developed a fine breed of horse called Robbins Roans.

Frank died at his home July 2, 1984. His death ended a career of wild horse running equal to none. Robbins estimated he had caught 25,000 to 30,000 wild horses in his day. It sounds like a lot of horses, but Frank Robbins was a lot of horse runner.

ABOUT THE AUTHOR

Jack Price rode in his first rodeo at Lake Campbell near Brookings, South Dakota, at age 10. He started out riding calves. It wasn't until the following summer that he tackled a big Brahman. The bull bucked him down as if he were a fly, but this didn't discourage the young cowboy from riding.

His father, Jake Price, moved his family to Wyoming when Jack was 12 years old. Jake and his five sons became involved in running and corralling wild horses in Fire Hole and on the Red Desert. Eventually, they worked with Frank "Wild Horse" Robbins.

After World War II, Jack farmed for 10 years and then drove a gasoline transport for 21 years. He is now retired and lives with his wife, Mavis, in Revillo, South Dakota. Jack is active in the campaign to preserve the wild mustang.

Jack Price

ISBN 1-57579-160-9